Five drivers.
One race.
Millions of tentacles.

It is the year 2025. Ten years ago, the United States of America strong-armed its way into another world war but this time it found itself on the losing end, ravaged by nuclear, chemical, and biological weapons. The rest of the countries of the world are now working to rebuild civilization, collectively shunning the USA. Now the inhabitants of America are at the mercy of mutants, freaks, marauders, gangs, and the most powerful warlord gangster in the country, the mysterious Mr. Silver.

PROLOGUE

The house was partially destroyed and looked extremely unsafe but Chaps didn't care. He dug through the rubble that served as a front door and crawled into the building. His friend Ryan was right behind him, rubbing his hands in anticipation.

"You think there's anything good left?" Ryan said.

"Shit, there better be. Last five houses we hit were empty as hell. This one's gotta have something. It's the biggest one on the block. Right now I'd settle for a fucking TV Guide."

"Well," Ryan said, tripping on a black block of wood, "I figure if we don't score anything here, we should move on to Hackensack."

"Yeah." Chaps walked through what resembled a living room except the furniture looked like ancient artifacts. He was used to scavenging for supplies but they had hit a period of bad luck recently.

He put his hands on the couch but quickly pulled them away; the fabric was warm and moist. Though he'd seen it many times, Chaps never got used to the effect the war had had on fabric. He found it strange that inorganic materials had been affected so much. But maybe it made sense. It hadn't been just nuclear weapons used in the war. A lot of biological and chemical shit was used by all sides of the conflict. He had heard how some woman spent the night on a couch and woke up with the fabric melded to her body. She had to cut herself off it with a piece of aluminum, losing much of her skin in the process.

Chaps didn't want that to happen to him so he never slept on anything but dirt. Even then, you never knew what was in the soil. There could be radioactive worms or something. Just the thought of nuclear creepy-crawlers made him shiver.

He carefully grabbed the couch again and said, "Help me turn this shit over quick." Ryan took hold of the other side and they flipped it.

"Jesus."

Underneath was a crude decagram made of green bones and Matchbox cars.

"Grab those cars. We can probably trade them," Chaps said. He wasn't really particular when it came to looting. From his experience he had learned that no matter what it was, there was someone in the wasteland who wanted it. One time he had pocketed a pouch full of old grocery store coupons. Despite their being useless after the war, Chaps had found a woman who offered him sex in exchange for them. The coupons held some psychological value to her, something she could use to pretend the world hadn't changed, hadn't turned to shit. Though he couldn't really relate to that, Chaps had taken her up on her offer. He had gotten some bizarre disease as a result. His teeth were never the same.

Ryan grabbed the cars and stuffed them into his pockets.

"What about the bones?" Ryan said.

"What about them? If you want 'em, you take 'em."

Ryan shook his head.

They continued to ransack the house, finding nothing else but a shower curtain.

"We can use this," Chaps said.

"For what?"

"As a poncho, you know? When it rains."

"It's moldy as hell," Ryan said, grabbing a corner of the curtain and sticking into his friend's face. "It looks alive or something."

"Beggars can't be choosers, man. It doesn't take up much room anyway," Chaps said. When he grabbed the shower curtain, he realized just how moldy it truly was. He wasn't going to admit that to Ryan, of course. Once he made a decision, Chaps stood by it. The curtain felt alive in his hands like a flattened tentacle.

After their search, they walked outside and sat on the curb. "Some toys and a shower curtain. What a haul," Ryan said. "We don't catch some better luck soon, we're going to be in bad shape."

"Yeah, I know."

"Maybe we should have taken those bones."

"Green bones? Anyone ever ask us if we had green bones? You think people want to trade for them?"

Ryan shrugged. "I heard you can get high off Yugg bones."

"Who the hell said they were Yugg bones?"

"No one, I'm just saying. They looked weird. Maybe we could crush them and, you know, smoke them."

"Don't be a freak, Ryan."

A sound from behind the house startled them.

"What the hell was that?" Ryan said.

"Shhhh!" Chaps put his hand up. "Shut up."

There was another sound like someone dragging empty

cans. Chaps pulled his knife out of his belt and walked towards the noise, which was getting louder. A figure walked out from behind the house.

"Christ! It's Mario," Chaps said. He turned to the man walking towards them. "What the hell are you trying to do? Scare us to death?"

A short, swarthy man with a handlebar mustache walked over to Chaps and Ryan, grinning ear to ear. "Aye, well, thought you'd hear me coming with all these cans, yeah."

"Why are you carrying those around?" Ryan said.

"I don't know, really. Just found them along the way and thought they sounded nice."

"Well, you sure as hell can't sneak up on anybody," Ryan said.

Mario laughed. "Guess not. Hey, you guys hear about the race?"

Chaps said, "Yeah, but I didn't think that was real. Sounds like a fucking joke."

"Naw, it's for real, bud."

Ryan piped in. "What race?"

Mario lowered his voice and talked slowly. "Mr. Silver's holding a race for the best drivers around."

"No shit?" Ryan said, "Silver?"

"Yeah, Silver," Mario said, "It starts at his compound in Jersey City and goes all the way down to Atlantic City. Real hardcore shit, you know. Kill or be killed."

Chaps said, "I heard the winner's gonna get as much gasoline as they can fit in their gas tank, plus supplies. Food, water, whatever."

"Shit," Ryan said. "But who's going to trust Silver? He's a gangster. A maniac."

"Rich maniac, remember," Mario said. "But he does follow through with his promises. Remember last year's race between Sabbath and Chainsaw Cook? Sabbath won a car, bud. I saw it."

"I heard something else, though. Something about a new city," Chaps said.

Mario's face turned grim. "Yeah. I heard about that, too. A city that rose from the sea or something."

Ryan laughed. "What? You mean like Atlantis? Man, that shit's fake like UFOs and Bigfoot."

"No, not Atlantis," Mario said. He lowered his voice again. "R'lyeh."

"Never heard of it," Ryan said.

"I heard it's a bad place, bud."

Chaps said, "Well, I heard it's a fucking paradise. The winner gets to live there."

Mario shook his head. "Not a paradise, bud. Not a paradise."

"Well," Ryan said. "If I had a motherfucking car, I'd enter that race."

"It's an invite-only deal," Chaps said. "Silver sent one of his guys to recruit the best racers from every race ever raced."

"No shit?"

"Yeah," Chaps said. He turned away from his friends and walked out to the edge of the road. "You guys hear that?"

"What?" Ryan said.

"Sounds like a car."

Mario stood up. "Marauders?"

"I don't know."

"Maybe it's a trade bus," Ryan said.

"Shhhhhhhh!"

They stood silently, perking their ears up to hear the sound. In the distance, the rough purr of an engine echoed.

Soon they saw it: a car, sleek and dusty and coming up fast on the horizon.

Ryan said, "Better get out of the way." He moved towards the house and the other men followed. They stood on the porch, watching as the car approached, interested in the possibility of someone new to bargain with.

Ryan squinted and tried focusing on the vehicle as it got closer. "Looks serious."

"What do you mean?" Chaps said.

"Doesn't look like a wanderer."

"Shit, bud," Mario said. "I think we should leave. I'm getting some bad vibes, you know."

"Nah, just wait." Chaps walked across the lawn. He wasn't worried about one car on an empty road.

The car approached and slowed while passing the house.

The three men caught a glimpse of the driver: a very beautiful blonde woman in her late twenties. She winked as she drove by.

"Wow," Ryan said.

"Wow indeed," Mario said. "This is one time I really wish I had a car."

"Do you even know how to drive?" Chaps said.

"No but I'd learn, bud. For *her* I'd learn."

The car drove a half-mile down the road and whipped around in the parking lot of a burnt-down convenience store.

"She's coming back." Chaps stepped out to the edge of the road. It had been so long since he had been close to an attractive female—or any female for that matter. As the car drove back towards the house, Chaps felt his heart flutter in anticipation.

Maybe this chick was in heat. Maybe he could have a crack at her.

Ryan called for him. "Dude, get the hell back here."

"No, just wait. She's slowing down," Chaps said, taking a few steps into the road to flag her down.

"I'm serious, man. Get the hell over here." Ryan jogged off to the road and pulled Chaps back.

"What the hell....?"

Before Chaps could finish his sentence, the car that had been slowing down was speeding in their direction. He was in mid-scream when metal hit flesh and bone.

With engine roaring, it plowed through Chaps and Ryan. It was quick and painful, body parts and blood burst into a rainbow of gore.

Windshield wipers fluttered quickly to clean up the mess.

Mario was standing in front of the house but, as the two friends were mown down, he turned and ran through the backyard making his way through the overgrown grass. The car followed.

Mario didn't make it very far. It was seconds before the car nipped the back of his knees in a blur of cracked bone, causing the man to fall forward. The car didn't hesitate. It quickly separated Mario's head from his body, sending it onto the hood of the car where it sat staring through the glass.

The driver cackled. "Get the hell off my car, asshole." She slammed on the brakes. Mario's head rolled off the hood and fell into a patch of toxic grass and bulbous mushrooms.

With screeching tires the car sped back to the street. The girl inside put a cell phone to her ear and said, "Oh my god, can you believe those guys? What a bunch of losers, digging through garbage. What's that? I can't hang out tonight. I told you, I'm going to that race. Yeah. Well, I'll call you later, sweetie, okay?"

She nodded and listened. "I miss you, too."

But there was no one on the other line. Cell phones hadn't worked since the war.

"Okay, I'll call you when I get to the race," the girl said and placed the phone on the passenger seat.

She stepped on the gas and brought the car up to its maximum speed. She was going to be late for the race. It was all because of those guys at the house. She almost regretted stopping to snuff them out but then realized it had been good practice. Her car sped off North. She was on her way to a race.

A death race.

TENTACLE
DEATH TRIP

ERASERHEAD PRESS
205 NE BRYANT STREET
PORTLAND, OR 97211

WWW.ERASERHEADPRESS.COM

ISBN: 978-1-62105-025-4

TENTACLE
DEATH TRIP

JORDAN KRALL

Eraserhead Press
Portland, OR

For Jonah

CHAPTER ONE

Howdy, race fans! I'm your humble host Enzo. You will not believe the exciting spectacle you are about to witness. Mr. Silver himself, yes, that Mr. Silver, has put together the best race you'll ever see.

I know what you're thinking. You're saying, "Enzo, what about the race between Sabbath and Chainsaw Cook? What about the three-way between Cane Toad Moon, Meat Sham Bo, and the Laird? Well let me tell you, people, those races are nothing compared to what's coming up. I can assure you! This will be one for the record books!

The rumble of the engine made Samson nervous.

He felt this way despite having won two dozen races against some of the fiercest competitors. He beat Razor Mays and Macronympha Phil in Baltimore. He had left plenty of racers in his dust within the last few years. But this race was different.

Samson sat looking out the freshly-washed windshield, waiting for the race to begin, a death race, a gory opiate for the masses. There he was revving his engine in Mr. Silver's Northern Compound, one of two places the warlord gangster called home and the starting point of the race. Situated in Jersey City, New Jersey, it was a stadium constructed out of concrete blocks, truck skeletons, and random pieces of industrial plastic.

Samson looked over at the other drivers. There were supposed to be four other than himself but he only saw three. The driver to his immediate left was a plump, older woman in a souped-up minivan. Her body was wide, her neck short and fat. Her red hair sat on top of her head like a dead fox. The woman was inspecting her engine when she looked up and made eye contact with Samson. She stuck out her tongue and wiggled it obscenely.

Samson was startled when an emaciated man in the audience screamed at the woman, "Fat bitch!" The man stood up and grabbed his crotch with his dirty, mangled hand.

The plump racer pulled a flare gun from her waistband and pulled the trigger. A bright flash left the muzzle of the gun and landed on the man's face. He screamed as the skin on his face melted off into his hands.

The audience cheered.

Samson turned his eyes away from the gory scene and looked to his right where a small Japanese woman was sitting on a small two-door car. Something wasn't right about the woman, though. Samson squinted and looked at her legs. They were hairy.

It wasn't a Japanese woman. It was a man. He was wearing so much make-up that he resembled a slutty, underdressed Kabuki actress. There was a handcuff on each of his wrists but the chain that had connected them was dangling. As Samson watched, the Japanese man grabbed a small fistful of his own hair and ate it.

Samson turned away with a shudder and got out of his

car to get a better look around. Next to the cross-dresser was a muscle car convertible Samson couldn't identify. It resembled a Corvette but there was something wrong about it. The driver, a beefy, half-naked man with a Mohawk, was even stranger. His skull was made of glass, his brain and eyeballs visible through it, floating in what looked like gasoline. Two leather straps crisscrossed his chest and on his shoulders were large metal spikes. He looked more like a steroid-infused gladiator than a racer.

Samson wondered where the fifth driver had gone. He got back into his car and that's when he heard the engine behind him.

A blue Camaro IROC-Z sped down the road and entered the arena. Samson watched as the fifth racer pulled up next to the plump old woman in the minivan. Inside was a young, blonde girl chatting on a cell phone.

The crowd of spectators cheered as a bullhorn sounded through the compound and one of the video screens flickered on. Silver's face appeared on the screen looking fox-like and well-fed. He wore a short ponytail and a gold chain with a sun-shaped pendant.

He said, "Hello drivers and race fans, I'm Mr. Silver and I welcome you to the greatest race of your lives." With that the crowd cheered louder, not only because of Silver's words but because some of his men began to throw small packets of dried meat into the audience. No one but Silver knew exactly what *kind* of meat it was but Samson was sure he didn't want to know. The people didn't seem to care. They were poor and desperate for some sustenance to go with their bloody entertainment. Their lives consisted mostly of survival and Silver's diversion was a bright point in their somber existences.

Through the loudspeakers, Silver went on, "I've always lived by the rule: if you get, you give. I've always gotten a lot of enjoyment from races. The roar of the engines, the suspense as the drivers make their way around the track. It is one of life's greatest thrills. Because I've gotten that, I'm going to give it back by staging one of the most spectacular races ever imagined." The pony-tailed gangster chuckled.

Samson watched the other racers, their eyes were glued on Silver's face. They looked enthralled as if the race was the best thing that had ever happened to them.

"But as in every game, there are rules!" Silver said. "First, you cannot leave New Jersey and drive through the Western Wastelands. I consider that a blatant show of disrespect. I'm a man of respect if nothing else. You should understand that leaving New Jersey is an instant disqualification. You will be killed on sight."

He snickered. "There is only one stop permitted, a gas station in Hell's Fish Market. You cannot attack the other drivers while at the station. This is very important. Consider it a safe zone. Once they leave the station, you may commence the violence. Elsewhere, you may maim, burn, kill, and destroy anyone or anything in your way except for *my* people. The more violence the better the entertainment and that's what the audience is here for. And another thing you must remember: *you have an audience.* As a driver in my race your life is no longer your own. You are not living your life in isolation. I have cameras nearly everywhere and everything will be broadcast here for your fans and for your fans that are waiting so patiently in my Atlantic City compound. They deserve a show. Never forget that. They deserve a show!"

The crowd cheered but Samson laughed softly, quiet enough

that he didn't think anyone had heard him.

He was wrong.

A hulking man wearing nothing but a leather mask and a codpiece walked up to Samson's window and bent over so his head was inside the car. Samson smelled smoke and fish. The man said nothing but he didn't need to. Samson could see his eyes: milky white marbles with just a speck of black in the middle. They told him everything he needed to know.

"Sorry," Samson said, trying to transform his fear into machismo and staring down the man, knowing he'd lose in that silent contest. The milk-eyed man pulled his head out of the car and stood up. The word COP was drawn on his chest in blood.

Silver's voice brought Samson to attention. "Oh, and Cop over there is my number one enforcer. He'll meet you down in Atlantic City. Let's give a round of applause for Cop!"

Again the crowd cheered as Cop bowed slowly and waved like a drugged automaton.

"And now for the part everyone has been waiting for…just in case you have forgotten why you are here. The prizes. Oh, the wonderful, wonderful prizes. You may or may not have heard there has been a historical milestone down south off the coast of Atlantic City. Something timeless and quite beautiful has risen from the depths of the ocean. Those who know their history may know about R'lyeh, the beautiful city, an ageless paradise. It is your home if you win the race. You'll have to share it with me, of course. You will become my business partner in a sense, helping to organize future races and all that. I need the best racer, the one with the most expertise, one willing to risk their life for me. The winner will be crucial in the rebuilding of this, the new age of our civilization. Oh, the fun we'll have!"

Silver laughed and so did the audience. "And in addition to that, you'll get all the gas, food, and water you'll ever need."

Samson heard the other racers cheer but he stayed silent.

"To keep the audience abreast of the race, my man Enzo will be acting as announcer. He'll be giving a play by play. Enzo, are you ready?" Silver's face on the video screen made mock movements as if he could really see through the screen.

A short man in a white suit ran out from behind the cars. "Right here, boss!" Enzo said into a microphone. His voice boomed through the arena. "I'm ready." He waved at the audience. "Are YOU ready?"

The crowd roared.

Silver clapped his hands. "Then let's introduce the drivers!"

CHAPTER TWO

Now let's take a look as the racers are getting ready, revving their engines, and preparing for the race of their lives… possibly their deaths!

First up we have the beautiful but dangerous Gabby Peppermint in her equally beautiful Camaro. Yowzah! What a looker! I'm sure it's well-equipped with all sorts of nasty things for her competitors. And yes, that was Ms. Peppermint showing up a tad late but you know: beauty takes time!

Next we have Mama Hell who comes to us all the way from the Bible Belt Wasteland. Don't let her motherly looks fool you…she's a vicious driver! And that minivan is much, much more than your average suburban vehicle. Looks can be deceiving. Watch out!

And then we have the mysterious Samson in his custom built Ligotti Turbo Z-23, one of the fastest cars around. And you young ladies out there, doncha think he's pretty handsome for an older man? Yowzah! But hands off…he doesn't strike me as the sort of guy who lets anyone get too close!

Speaking of ladies…next is Junko, a cute little he/she in a souped-up 1987 Honda Civic Si. What a classic! Now Junko himself (or herself!) is a firecracker who'll burn you just as soon as look at you.

Last but certainly not least we have the legend himself, Drac Dunwich, hailing from the Bronx where for the last year he's made a name for himself in the small circuit races. Now, with that glass skull of his, Drac is quite the spectacle. Yowzah! And don't get too close to him...he's a thirsty fella! I'm sure you'll see...

*

Samson revved his engine and hoped they'd get on with it. He wasn't interested in all the pomp and ceremony. His stomach was in knots. He wanted to start the race. He *needed* to start the race.

While the audience chanted Silver's name, Samson wondered about Drac Dunwich. He had heard the name before, heard some of the stories, but had no idea he was participating in the race. The nervousness Samson had felt bumped up a notch. Was it true Drac had won a race against Navajo Willie and then slaughtered him after the race, for the pleasure of the bloodthirsty audience? Rumor had it Drac still had Willie's teeth in the glove compartment of his car.

Samson heard Enzo's voice echo through the arena, giving a short rundown of the general route they were about to take. Then Enzo said, "Drivers! On your marks! This is the moment you've been waiting for. Yowzah! Get ready!"

The crowd screamed. Samson thought they looked ready to riot, to tear up the whole compound in an orgy of excitement. Were they going to be satisfied with just a race? Sooner or later Silver would have to provide them with something else, something more than fast cars and faster death.

But what else was there?

Dressed in a white tuxedo and wearing a pencil-thin

mustache, Enzo stepped onto a stage and danced around in front of the video screen that now displayed a still shot of Silver's face. Enzo pointed wildly at the drivers.

"Go!"

Then Enzo pulled down his white pants and defecated on the stage to wild cheers from the audience.

CHAPTER THREE

Samson's car shot out from the starting line like an angry bullet.

In his rearview mirror, he kept an eye on the other cars as they followed. Drac was the first one to tail him and then come up along the side.

Samson looked over at the man, this legend he had heard so much about, and tried to get a look at his car. All cars now were custom-equipped with weaponry and that weaponry varied with the driver. It was good to know what kind of attacks the competition would be bringing with them.

The smell of dust and exhaust made Samson think of his time in the Wastelands but he shook those memories from his head and concentrated on the race. It was a clear road of asphalt and trash in front of him while Drac stayed alongside, not attempting to speed up and pass Samson.

"What are you up to, Dunwich?" Samson said. He sped up and Drac did the same. He looked over again and saw two eyes looking back at him, suspended in gasoline in a translucent skull in front of a brain that looked slightly smaller than it should have been.

Samson let up on the gas and fell back a few feet. He expected

Drac to follow suit but was surprised when he accelerated.

"Son of a bitch," Samson said, speeding up to tail Drac.

Junko and Mama Hell passed him on the left, veering off to enter Mouthville instead of riding into the Gears. It might be a smart move because despite Mouthville's unpredictable environment, it wasn't nearly as dangerous. Samson decided not to follow them. In his rearview mirror he saw Gabby Peppermint on his ass, chatting on her cell phone, looking oblivious to the race.

As he tried to move up front, Drac zigzagged to prevent him from doing so. The sides of the road were blocked with blocks of concrete but Samson could see he'd have a chance to pass up the road…if he was careful.

CHAPTER FOUR

Yowzah! I don't know about you folks but I think the race has got off to a good start. Samson shot out like a rocket, leading for a little bit until old Drac decided to take the position. So we have Drac in first place on his way to the Gears with Samson right behind him, Gabby close behind. Cute little Junko and Mama Hell followed a different route through Mouthville, bypassing the Gears. Did you see Mama run over that poor little puppy? Wow, she's really bloodthirsty today.

I.

Junko was excited.

This was his first race driving solo and it was as intense as he thought it would be, in the car alone, just him and the purring of the machine. That was something he had always dreamt about.

He'd had some worries, of course. Driving in high heels wasn't easy and he wished he'd brought a change of shoes. He couldn't drive barefoot. It hurt his feet and he didn't want to mess up his pedicure. Maybe he'd find a pair of shoes during the race. Weirder things have happened.

A cough erupted from his throat and a clump of hair and bile oozed onto his tongue. Junko swallowed it all back down.

He followed Mama Hell's minivan into Mouthville, a place that resembled a dusty forest. During the war it was a military training facility but had been overrun with mutated animals and radioactive dust.

"Okay, Mama bitch, here's where you get off!" Junko said, driving up and tapping the minivan on the left corner of its fender. He sped up to the other side and tapped it again.

Mama Hell stepped on the brakes and Junko took that opportunity to sneak up alongside the left and pass her, giving her the finger as he did so. "Fuck you!"

Junko left the minivan behind as he sped down the road, swerving to avoid the road kill. He was going to win this race for sure. He had to. If he won it, he'd get the respect he deserved. He had always had to stand behind someone else but not now, no.

As he passed the trees, Junko thought he saw something move between them. It was too big to be an animal or a person. If he didn't know better he would have thought it was a tornado.

He looked in his rearview and saw Mama Hell thirty-feet behind him. It didn't seem like she was even trying to get closer. What was she up to?

Junko saw the thing in the trees again but this time it rose up. It was approaching. It *was* a tornado. Junko started to hug the left side of the road but was worried that he'd be leaving Mama Hell enough room to pass by.

That's when the twister came straight for him, engulfing his car. It sounded like a million pebbles pelting the outside.

It was a tornado, yes, but there was something different about this one.

It was a tornado of *teeth*.

The small cyclone was twisting around Junko's car, scraping the paint off with its teeth of all shapes and sizes. Some were white teeth, some were yellow and brown but all were razor sharp. Soon he could hear the teeth biting into the metal and puncturing the plastic siding.

He stepped on the brakes and swerved over to the right, hitting Mama Hell's car as she tried to pass him and avoid the twister at the same time. The teeth still rocking his car, Junko saw flashes of light. He peered through the tooth tornado, that old bitch was shooting flares at him.

Junko sped up and swerved to the right to get in front of her and out of the tornado's way. After his third attempt he was successful but the flares kept coming and he started to smell something burning.

One of the old bitch's flares caught the top of his car and was burning a hole through the roof. He lifted himself off the seat, holding the wheel with one hand while trying to find the burn hole with the other. There it was right over the passenger's seat. He rummaged through his supplies and brought out a small pack of fireproof putty. He slapped some on the hole and brought his hand back to the wheel.

The teeth tornado was behind him now and so was Mama Hell. Junko stepped on the gas, trying to get as far away as possible, ignoring the road kill despite the fact that the bones of those mutant animals could do major damage to the underside of an automobile.

In his rearview mirror he saw Mama Hell try to drive out of the twister which was now engulfing her minivan. "Haha, you old bitch," Junko said. That woman thought she could disrespect him. He'd show her and everyone else.

II.

Six Months Ago

Sabbath bought Junko for ten gallons of gasoline and a motorcycle equipped with a chainsaw.

Junko thought he was worth more but that's all Sabbath was willing to dish out for a Japanese transvestite sex slave. Such was life after the war. Weak flesh was bought and sold, used as currency among the degenerate or the desperate. Body Stations were set up throughout the wasteland where people could buy, sell, and trade humans weaker than themselves. Men, women, children: nothing was off limits.

Ten years ago, the war had left Junko a twelve-year-old orphan. But he wasn't going to dwell on that loss or let it get in the way of his survival. When he saw the man who had bartered for him, Junko wasn't pleased. Sabbath was one of the most grotesque looking men he'd ever seen. But Junko was going to be a winner and if that meant giving blowjobs to a deformed giant who drove a truck full of radioactive goats, then so be it.

The torture seemed endless. Sabbath was an oversexed brute who was intent on defiling his new slave in every way possible. Within a week, Sabbath had practically destroyed Junko's rectum. They had had to bring in a man named Doctor Solange who did a sloppy surgery and widened Junko's anus until it resembled a vagina. Sabbath was happy with the result. Doctor Solange accepted payment in the form of being able to take the first crack at the modified hole.

The torture wasn't just sexual, either. Junko was beaten with fists, pipes, and baseball bats. He was cut with swords, knives, and car parts. Most of the time he had only Sabbath's urine to drink, occasionally mixed with water or fruit juice. His food consisted of whatever meat had spoiled so much that Sabbath wouldn't eat it himself. Sometimes the meals included feces and shredded leather topped with phlegm. Junko soon learned to eat everything with relish because if there was any hesitation or show of distaste for what Sabbath gave him, a brutal beating was inevitable.

After years, Junko had come to terms with his position as Sabbath's sex slave and map reader. He fulfilled his duties obediently until he heard the two words that would change everything.

"Jap cunt!" Sabbath said.

Hearing those two words was an epiphany to Junko. He'd been called each of them separately but their being combined made him realize just how Sabbath saw him.

"Yes?"

"Wake the fuck up. We gotta go to Columbus and race Drunky Booster. You lean your head over here in case I gotta piss, got it?"

Junko nodded and laid his head down on his master's lap. He was handcuffed to the steering wheel. "I'm all yours, Sabbath."

"Nothing but a Jap cunt, you know that? Piece of shit," Sabbath said, sending a fist down on the side of Junko's head. He started the car and pulled out onto the road, speeding down the deserted highway.

"Yes, Sabbath." Junko smirked. He had dreamt about earning his freedom, earning his right to move from the passenger seat to the driver's. Sabbath had always told him that Japs couldn't drive but Junko knew that wasn't true.

"What the hell you smiling for, bitch?" Another fist landed on Junko's temple.

"Nothing."

"You better tell me or I'll beat your ass," Sabbath growled. "You don't want to know what happened to my last slave."

"Oh, but I do," Junko said and then bit down on Sabbath's leg. Not bad for a Jap cunt.

"Fuck!"

It was a good thing Sabbath only wore a codpiece, as many marauders after the war. Junko was biting directly into flesh.

The car swerved into a concrete divider but Junko pulled the steering wheel straight, biting down harder. He ignored the fists as they pummeled his head, neck, and back. Sabbath even pulled at Junko's hair, tearing clumps right out of his skull. There was pain, yes, but the pain turned pleasurable because he knew he was enduring it for a reason. It was for freedom.

Sabbath stepped on the brakes and the car spun across the road. Junko's teeth didn't budge and soon his mouth was inches deep in leg meat.

Junko's loose hand flew up to Sabbath's neck and his glittery fingernails dug into his jugular, opening a fountain of blood all over the dashboard. The big man gargled and took his hands off the wheel. Junko pulled his mouth out of the thigh flesh.

"What did you do to your last slave, Sabbath?" Junko asked the bleeding hulk.

"Baaaabaaaaaaapffffffftttttttttttt!"

"WHAT DID YOU DO TO HIM?"

Sabbath looked him in the eyes and said, "Gave him a lupara enema..."

Junko had heard Sabbath talk about the lupara enema from time to time, putting a sawed off shotgun to someone's ass and pulling the trigger. Junko dug his fingers deeper into the man's neck. It was over for Sabbath.

Junko managed to stop the car, dump the body, and find the key to the handcuffs. Instead of taking them completely off, he separated the cuffs and wore them to remind himself of what he had endured. Wearing the jewelry of his freedom, Junko would never be dominated again.

He drove the car back to Sabbath's place, a small fortress in a junkyard, and started packing supplies into the Honda Civic he had been working on in the little free time Sabbath had given him. That's when the armored limousine pulled up and a short man walked up to the gate.

"Hey! You there in the dress! Is Sabbath here?"

Junko put his hand on a small sword and said, "Why? Who are you?"

"I'm a representative of Mr. Silver."

Junko had heard about Silver: a gangster warlord taking advantage of people after the war. He was the one who organized some of Sabbath's races and ran the body stations.

"I work for Mr. Sabbath. What do you want?"

The man tapped on the gate. "Can I come in?" Junko nodded and walked over to let him in, the sword still at his side.

Junko said, "What's this about?"

"If you don't mind, I'd like to talk directly to Sabbath about it. No offense to you, miss," he said, eying Junko's legs.

"Well, how about you tell me and I'll put in a good word for you." Junko winked at the man knowing his sex appeal was going to win the conversation. He rubbed the back of his hand on the man's crotch. "So how about it?"

"Yowzah…."

And that's how Junko entered the race in lieu of Sabbath.

GABBY

CHAPTER FIVE

Yowzah! What an exciting race so far with Junko and Mama Hell getting caught in a teeth storm and making it out in the nick of time. While they're trying to get through Mouthville, the rest of the racers are entering the Gears and you know what that means! The gear bugs will be out in droves, ready to put a glitch in our racers' plans. It looks like Drac Dunwich and Samson are head to head but young hotshot Gabby Peppermint is closing in.

I.

Gabby Peppermint was already sick of the race.

In particular she was sick of the other drivers. To her they were just nobodies, trying to take what she deserved. It was the story of her life: people cheating her out of what was rightfully hers, stealing the spotlight from her, trying to make their pathetic lives important.

She kept her Camaro at a constant speed because she wanted to let the two dumb-asses in front of her fight it out. She'd study their driving and figure a way to exploit their weaknesses. People always thought she was stupid because she was blonde but Gabby knew she had brains behind the beauty.

She was going to use those brains to kill these assholes and win the race.

Gabby had never driven through the Gears before; it looked like a shit-hole, like a giant junkyard. Houses were covered in metal, car parts, faded porcelain signs, and unidentifiable jetsam. It reminded Gabby of the pathetic garage sales her mom always dragged her to as a child.

While she kept her eyes on Drac and Samson, something jumped out in front of her car. Gabby swerved but hit it anyway.

"Oh my god, what the hell?" Why did everything have to be so difficult? She was sick of things getting in the way of her happiness.

Whatever she had hit had flipped up onto the top of her car. A face dropped down in front of the windshield. Gabby screamed but it was more out of frustration than fear.

It was a gear bug, a victim of radioactivity. Where limbs should have grown but didn't, mechanical parts were attached. This one in particular had a sprocket instead of a left eye and a head full of wire instead of hair. His fingers were rusty copper talons.

"Get off my car, asshole!" Gabby swerved across the road, trying to shake the gear bug off but it held on. The thing was slowly making its way to the passenger side window.

Gabby slammed on the brakes and the gear bug flew off onto the road in front of her. She put her car into park and screamed.

That freak on the road was going to die. She wasn't going to let some asshole make a fool of her in front of everybody. People were watching her, expecting her to be the winner, the princess, the only one who deserved any attention.

She was the only Sweet Sixteen.

Gabby reached into the backseat and stepped out of the car. In her hands was a pink sledgehammer. "Hey, asshole!" She ran up to the gear bug scrambling to stand up despite its injuries.

Gabby heaved the hammer over her shoulder and sent it flying into the bug's face. Its head exploded. Blood, skull, oil, and wire sprinkled the asphalt. From behind her, Gabby heard metallic footsteps. More gear bugs were approaching.

"Come on, fuckers!"

At her words, they ran out like hungry roaches, scurrying around her. Gabby's face was red, her hands trembling with fury. There was no way those assholes were leaving alive. If they took one step near her, they were all going to be crushed.

One ran forward, obviously a woman, with a ribcage made of steering wheel parts. She whistled through plastic teeth. Her metallic face flattened as the sledgehammer hit.

Another gear bug ran up behind Gabby and cut her with a rusty fish-shaped piece of metal. Gabby elbowed him and gave a quick jab with the hammer that exposed flesh stitched together with fine wire. She jabbed again, this time with more power. His chest caved in. One more hit and he was squealing towards death.

The three remaining gear bugs were reluctant now. Gabby taunted them, daring them to come nearer. She knew they were too scared, that they were just trying to save face by sticking around. With a scowl she walked back to her car and sped away.

"Better luck next time, assholes!" she screamed out the window. She almost wished they had attacked her. It would have been sweet to kill a few more worthless pieces of shit. She just hoped the audience liked her performance. She hoped there were a lot of cameras around catching that action. If there weren't, someone would have to pay with their lives. After all, she never exerted herself for nothing. She deserved all the attention. She deserved to be a star.

II.

Ten Years Ago

It was on the eve of her Sweet Sixteen Party when the news hit: all the major nations in the world were preparing for war.

Nuclear war.

The United States. China. North Korea. Pakistan. India. Great Britain. Hell, even Japan was throwing its hat in the ring despite its tragic history with nukes.

Gabby couldn't care less. War or no war, it didn't matter to her. What mattered was that it took the attention away from her big day. She was turning sixteen. Sweet Sixteen! But now everyone was talking about the war and how it could be the end of the world.

Who fucking cared, right?

Her parents had planned a huge party for her. They had rented a hall and everything. A limo was going to pick Gabby up and take her to the party while her friends watched in awe as she showed off the eight-hundred dollar dress her father had bought her.

She knew some of her friends talked behind her back, calling her a spoiled brat and "daddy's little princess" but what good was a father if he wasn't going to buy her things? After all, she'd given her parents the gift of having such a beautiful daughter so the least they could do was give her what she wanted, even if that meant accruing monstrous debt. But Gabby wasn't concerned. It was *their* debt and they shouldn't have had kids if they didn't want to max out their credit cards.

Gabby had woken up that morning, smiling at the thought that it was her sixteenth birthday and the whole day would be all about her. It wouldn't be about her friends, her little sister, her grandparents, her parents, or anyone else in the whole world. It would be her day and hers alone. No one was going to change that. But if they tried, she'd throw a fit.

"Mom! I want a cappuccino!" she yelled from her bed. There was no answer. "Mom!"

She wanted to sleep in, have breakfast in bed, and relax before getting ready for her party. But where was her mother? She should be standing at the foot of the bed awaiting Gabby's orders.

"Mom!" she yelled louder. "MOM!"

There was still no answer but this time Gabby heard muffled voices. Now she knew what was happening. Her family was planning to surprise her. Gabby quickly fixed her hair and sat up in bed, waiting for them to come in with a full gourmet breakfast and the first round of gifts.

She waited for ten minutes but no one came.

"MOM!"

Fuck, she'd just have to go downstairs to see what the hell was keeping them from giving her the attention she deserved. She stepped out of bed angrily, making sure to stomp on the floor loud enough so her family could get ready for the shit storm she was going to unleash.

When she got to the living room, she saw her parents and

sister huddled by the television watching a news report.

"What the hell's going on?" Gabby said. "You people don't even come up to wish me a happy birthday? It's my Sweet Sixteen!"

Her mother turned around and put her finger to her mouth. "Shhhhh! Look."

On the television there were images of mushroom clouds, rubble, bodies in wheel barrels, people crying, politicians shaking their heads, solemn newscasters, protests, planes dropping bombs, and other short clips of destruction.

"What's going on?" Gabby said, walking up behind her family. "You're watching the news? On my birthday? It's my Sweet Sixteen!"

Her dad turned around, "Gabriella, quiet!"

Gabby grunted, "Losers." She went into the kitchen but instead of the elaborate breakfast she expected to find, she found half-eaten toast. She stomped her foot and started rummaging through the kitchen.

The volume on the television got louder. *"North Korea retaliated, dropping an as yet unidentified biological weapon over Manhattan...."*

Gabby's mother gasped. She turned to her husband and saw his eyes widen in horror. But it wasn't the horror on the television he was reacting to. It was the knife severing his throat.

The birthday girl stood behind him, using a kitchen knife to saw her father's head off. Her mother and sister screamed, falling backward in shock. Gabby pulled the blade away and stabbed it down into her mother's face.

Her parents were bleeding out on the floor while her little sister cried hysterically, scooting away backwards on the floor.

"Gabby, Gabby! What are you doing?"

"Shut up, Tara!" She jumped on her little sister and sat on her chest. "Mom and Dad were losers. Can't you see? It's my Sweet Sixteen and what were they doing? They were watching the fucking news!"

As she straddled Tara, she felt something in her pocket. "What's this?" Gabby pulled something out. "You used my iPod? Again? I told you to keep your fucking hands off it!"

Gabby pulled the headphones off the iPod and wrapped them around her sister's throat, squeezing and squeezing until the girl turned blue. She let go of the wire and let her sister catch a breath.

"Thank you," Tara whispered. Tears gathered in her eyes.

"For what?" Gabby said. She tightened her grip on the headphone wires and started to squeeze again. Gabby's face became a deep red as she killed her little sister. "It's my Sweet Sixteen!"

After disposing of her family in the cellar, she called her friends but no one picked up. Was everyone abandoning her on her special day?

She prepared her own breakfast, something she had never done before. It was strange but she did the best she could and sat down in front of the television.

"Shit!" she said as she realized there was nothing on except news reports. In frustrated rage, Gabby put in a DVD of *Sex and the City*.

She thought of her dead family downstairs and mumbled, "It's my Sweet Sixteen."

MAMA HELL

CHAPTER SIX

Well, I said it once but I'll say it again: Yowzah!

The young and beautiful Gabby Peppermint really went bat-shit crazy and now she's on her way through the Gears. I'm fairly sure the gear bugs won't be messing with her again, don't ya agree?

And Mama Hell, well, she's trying to get through Mouthville in one piece after eating Junko's dust. I'm eager to see how she does it. Will the sweet lil' Mama make it or will she crash and burn?

Let's find out!

I.

"Stupid yellow slut," Mama Hell said, watching Junko speed forward, leaving her in the midst of the teeth tornado.

She didn't have anything personal against the other drivers except for that Jap. In fact, that other driver, that Samson guy, he was cute. If she was ten years younger, Mama thought she'd make a move on him.

Maybe not.

Men were dogs, plain and simple. They couldn't be trusted. Sure, they could provide a home, put food on the table, and do small home repairs but when it came down to it, they were good for little else. They sure didn't satisfy any emotional needs and rarely did any men satisfy her sexual needs. If you were lucky enough to find one man who could fuck well, he'd only keep it up until he was bored with you or got too old to put forth the energy.

Yep, men weren't worth the trouble.

But that was okay with Mama Hell. She was content racing. In her spare time she liked to help out the young people she encountered on her travels through the Wastelands, especially the women. The young men could fend for themselves. Back when her husband Nate was alive they had helped dozens of young women move to safe havens.

Mama Hell felt like she deserved something for herself, something that at least resembled retirement in the post-war era. Living in that city with Mr. Silver seemed like something she could deal with as long as Silver kept his distance.

She stepped on the gas, turned the wheel, and skidded out of the tornado, navigating the van around the grotesque tree branches that were scattered along the road. She realized they weren't branches but the bones of some nuclear wildlife.

As soon as she was close enough, Mama Hell pulled out another flare gun and shot it at Junko, who sped off even faster, getting out of the line of fire.

"Yellow freak!" Mama Hell said. She thought about how Junko was a man dressed as a woman. She considered herself a pretty tolerant and loving person but transvestites, homosexuals, and other sexual deviants were beyond her range of tolerance. They were sick abominations, blasphemous examples of what happens when society abandons God.

After the war, Mama had thought the devastation might

bring about change she could believe in. She hoped the riffraff, the outsiders, and the foreigners would die out, leaving the country to those who deserved it. She knew her ancestors came from Europe and weren't exactly native to the country but the Indians were as close to savages as you could get. They were worse than the Japs!

Things hadn't turned out like she wanted. The Wastelands were practically overrun with non-whites and she had a difficult time finding a good place to stay that didn't have too many blacks, Latinos, Indians, or some other variety of undesirables. Mama Hell hated how they roamed the land looking for handouts, robbing people…just like they did before the war. Whenever she got the chance, Mama ran some of them over or, if she felt creative, sent a flare at their heads to set those deadbeats on fire. She figured they needed to get used to fire as they'd be spending an eternity in it.

"Jap bastard."

Mama Hell was on Junko's tail. His little fag car was coughing exhaust in her face until there was a dust cloud in between them. "Son of a bitch," she said. It must have been intentional. That little Honda shouldn't be spitting out so much smoke.

Mama Hell couldn't see anything in front of her so she slowed down and crept up to Junko's right, only to have the bastard skid across to the side. The minivan hit a clump of road kill and almost went off the road. Mama got control and swung over to the other side of Junko, squeezing by fast enough to prevent him from blocking her. His little Honda tried to push her over but the minivan held its ground, refusing to budge.

Mama Hell opened up a compartment on her dashboard and pulled on a handle. A metal bar extended from the side of the minivan, attached to the end was a giant buzz saw. She pressed a button on the handle and the blade began to rotate.

She laughed. "Let's cut up a homo."

The buzz saw was almost touching Junko's car. The blade spun and as soon as Mama swung the minivan over to the left, it started cutting into the side of the Honda.

She wanted to bore that saw deep into the pansy car and cut that freak in half. Mama smiled at the thought of seeing blood and entrails spilling out from that ugly dress Junko wore. Then Mama would teach him another lesson with her steel-toed boots. Stomp, stomp, stomp. She'd crush his fruity little head like a melon.

The Honda tried to pull away but the buzz saw was embedded in the passenger side door. Mama's minivan wasn't going to let go that easily. Junko sped up and veered right, pulling the saw hard, bending the metal bar.

"Fucker," Mama Hell said, getting closer to Junko so her weapon wouldn't break. The saw was still boring into the Honda when it finally gave a jerk. She'd sawed through. If she could stay close enough to the Honda, she could cut that Jap in half.

But Junko had other plans. He braked and made an abrupt left turn, breaking the metal bar off the minivan entirely.

Mama Hell lost control for a few seconds, missing a huge chunk of glowing road kill by inches. "Shit!" she yelled, mourning the loss of her buzz saw. In the rearview mirror she saw Junko's car spin like a top, sparks and small metal shards flying through the air. She was tempted to go back and gut that stupid piece of shit right there in Mouthville but she knew that was too much of a risk. Who knows if that teeth tornado was coming back? It would be better to move on.

II.

One Year Ago

Mama and her husband Nate drove through the North Dakota wasteland, having an animated discussion about the merits of drinking one's own urine.

"I just think it's gross, Nate," Mama said.

"Soon it'll be the only way to survive, hon. You drink what water you can and then let it go through your system and then you drink it again. I know it sounds unappetizing but sooner or later, you'll have to do it."

His wife shook her head. "No way, not me."

Nate laughed, "We'll see." He slowed down the minivan, "Hey, look."

A young, topless woman was walking on the side of the road. Her hair was bright pink and she carried a bag full of bottle caps.

"Let's pull over," Nate said.

"I don't know."

"I thought you liked helping these girls out."

"She looks like a road whore to me. I don't trust the look of her."

"What would Jesus do, hon?"

Mama grunted, "I don't think he'd do what you have in mind!"

"What's *that* supposed to mean?" Nate pulled over.

"You know exactly what it means."

Nate turned the car off. "I'm just saying we've helped plenty of young women and it seems like simply because this one is half-naked and slightly, *slightly* more attractive than those dirt bags we usually pick up, you're jealous."

"Oh, go drink some piss, Nate," Mama said, crossing her arms and waiting for her husband to make his move. If he'd known what was best for him, he'd have kept on driving.

Nate stepped out of the car. Mama watched through the windshield as her husband approached the young woman carefully and started a conversation. From the looks of it, he was doing his best to play the role of a savior. Mama could just imagine the type of lies he was telling her, how he was a pastor (he hadn't been one in nine years) or how he had set up a homeless shelter before the war (he'd gotten as far as filling out the tax paperwork). That stupid girl probably believed it all.

After a few minutes the girl followed Nate back to the car. She smiled when she saw Mama. As she got into the backseat she said, "Hi, I'm Jane Mary."

"Well, well, how do you do, Jane Mary? I'm Sonia but people call me Mama."

The women shook hands as Nate got into the driver's seat with a goofy smile on his face.

"What are you smiling for, Nate?" Mama said.

He shrugged. "Oh, nothing."

Mama grunted. She could smell Jane Mary already. The road whore smelt like week-old sex stains and asphalt. It was only a matter of time until she made a move on Nate.

The three of them drove for several miles before they pulled over to the side of the road at a makeshift gas station. Post-war entrepreneurs sold synthetic gasoline that worked like shit but was enough to keep the car running. Rumors said the stuff was made from the blood of nuke mutants or Yuggs.

Nate said, "Hey Mama, want to stay here while I check out what they're selling? I think it'd be good if we stocked up."

"I'll stay here," Mama said, catching a quick glimpse at Jane Mary who was sleeping in the backseat. "Get me some juice if they have it."

"Sure thing, hon," Nate said. He walked towards a shed where a midget in homemade armor was holding a bag of corn. The armor was made out of cereal boxes and hubcaps spray-painted yellow. The two men exchanged words and then the little knight led Nate around the corner of the shed.

Mama heard a yawn from the back. Jane Mary stretched. "God, how long was I sleeping? Shit, I'm still beat."

"I don't know. An hour maybe."

"And I gotta piss like hell," she said, getting out of the minivan. "Need anything?"

"No, I'm fine," Mama said. She watched Jane Mary walk to the shed and look around. The girl inspected a few items: a turtle shell, a ceramic pot, a soiled magazine, yellow paperback books, purple jars. Then she walked around to the back of the shed.

A few minutes passed before Mama got suspicious. She knew something bad was going to happen the moment they picked up that road whore. Her father would have called this sense "Godly intuition," an instinct given by the Lord to his flock. He didn't want to tell them straight out what would happen. But he always gave clues and hints about the future to those who were willing to listen.

Mama got out of the car and walked over to the shed. She rummaged through some of the things for sale. She picked up a turtle shell. "I'll take this," she said to an ancient woman sitting on a chair made of Pepsi cans.

She walked around the shed and stepped straight into Hell.

Jane Mary was bent over a rusted keg. She was nude, exposing an elaborate red tattoo that covered her entire back. The armored midget was on a stepstool, thrusting his discolored penis into her mouth. Nate was on the other side, banging away at Jane Mary's backside. He grunted like an excited pig in slop.

Mama stared at the pornographic atrocity. Though she had expected something unsavory, she didn't think it was going to be so grotesque. The midget was banging his fists on the back of Jane Mary's head and the girl seemed to be enjoying it. Nate looked like he was in a trance, his eyes rolling up in his head as he wetted his penis in that road whore.

"What the hell?" Mama said, "Hell.......HELL!"

If she had envisioned torment everlasting, this would be it: gross betrayal by a loved one.

Nate didn't seem to hear her but the midget stopped moving and smiled. "You want in?"

That's when Mama rushed at them with the turtle shell. She slashed at Nate's face and neck. But he kept thrusting. It was as if he knew he was going to die but wanted to get one last orgasm before he did. Mama wasn't going to give him the satisfaction. She sent the turtle shell down to his penis, severing it inside Jane Mary's vagina.

Nate fell backwards, his groin spouting blood.

The midget laughed and pounded at Jane Mary, who was screaming through a mouthful of penis. Mama pushed her off the keg and fell on the midget. She stabbed at the little bastard's face, the sharpened turtle shell giving him a crude facelift.

Finally she turned to Jane Mary.

The girl was trembling on the ground, one hand in her crotch trying to extract the severed penis. Mama saw that the girl had tattoos on her chest as well as her back. She couldn't make out exactly what they were but it looked like a collage of screaming human faces, feet, octopi, a shovel, insects, and a cappuccino maker.

"You little whore," Mama said.

Jane Mary's fear turned into defiance. Her tattoos started to move, "You fat bitch."

Mama rushed at Jane Mary. She sat on her and punched her in the face, knocking her out. With the turtle shell, she dug into the girl's skin. Mama turned the whore over and continued. When she was done, she had stripped the slut of her tattooed skin.

The pain brought Jane Mary to consciousness and she started to scream. Mama put a foot down on her neck and slowly stepped down. Then she let go. The road whore wasn't going to die that easily. She was going to know the wrath of Mama.

She was going to know the wrath of Mama Hell.

CHAPTER SEVEN

Yowzah! What an amazing race! Mama Hell wasted no time in trying to get Junko out of the running. With her handy buzz saw she really did a number on his Honda but she failed to eliminate him. You can be sure Junko won't take that lying down!

Let's not neglect old Samson and Drac. They're making their way through the Gears. And boy, there seems to be a lot of tension there. I hope it's not sexual tension, haha! Just kidding, folks. Yowzah!

Samson was slightly ahead of Drac now, swerving slightly back and forth to prevent him from passing. Bizarre gunfire was echoing behind them, like the banging of a gong.

He sped up and glanced in his rearview mirror. Drac was standing up in his convertible. The car seemed to be steering itself. Samson thought it looked humorous, the big guy standing up proudly, his bare chest dripping with sweat, spiked shoulder pads and glass skull glistening in the sun. His mohawk was immobile, like it was made of plastic, not hair. Drac was holding up a white gun that looked like it was made of bone.

Samson wasn't worried about the gunfire but he wondered

what else Drac had planned. He thought about the post-war vehicles, each equipped with a small arsenal. Would it ever be safe enough to drive the streets without those weapons? And even if the world returned to normal, would people ever be willing to give up their razor chains, spinning saws, chainsaw hood ornaments, or trunks full of machine guns?

Drac was still shooting but not doing much damage. Then Samson noticed a strange shadow coming from the bottom of Drac's car.

Were those tentacles?

"Holy shit."

Dark green tendrils were moving out from under Drac's convertible and slowly snaking their way towards Samson's car.

Samson pushed a button between the seats. A cloud of white foam shot out of the trunk of his car, covering Drac.

Samson pushed his car to the limit, trying to get as far ahead as possible. He looked behind him and saw Drac go off the side of the road, into a field. He was relieved.

Then he saw the motorcycles.

They didn't look like any motorcycle he'd seen before. They were made of random machine parts, bleached bone, chains, melted plastic, and spikes. Each held a gear bug, deformed and frothing at the mouth with spittle and motor oil. If the rumors were true, they had only one purpose: to kill humans. They would use their bones as tools, and employ their flesh in occult-mechanical rituals.

Samson was surprised that they were able to keep up. The motorcycles looked like they were about to fall apart. One of them pulled up alongside him, giving Samson a closer look. Dressed in rags, the gear bug looked like a homeless robot.

Sprockets, wires, bulbs, and mechanical junk were thrown together haphazardly with deformed flesh. His eyes were two dull copper pieces. He opened a mouth full of black plastic.

Samson saw a spike extend from the cycle's wheel. The gear bug was trying to impale him. "Fuck you," Samson said. He hit the brakes, moved to the right, and bumped the cycle's back tire. It flipped and flew over Samson's car, exploding when it hit the ground.

Another gear bug was coming up fast on Samson's left side. This one was uglier than the first. He looked like a bundle of wires with a steel pumpkin for a head. A large bone spear appeared from beneath his overcoat. The gear bug hurled it towards Samson's window, cracking the glass.

Samson swerved to the right and then back to the left, bumping the gear bug off his motorcycle. The spear went flying through the air missing Samson's windshield by an inch.

"Holy shit," he said, speeding away from the wreckage and keeping an eye on the rearview. He was expecting Drac to appear any second. That foam wasn't going to stop him forever.

DRAC DUNWICH

CHAPTER EIGHT

Let's hear it for the gear bugs, huh? Those clever little buggers really gave Samson a run for his money. Yowzah!

And Drac Dunwich. Wow! How a man can drive standing up in his car is beyond me but somehow the man does it. No wonder he's a legend! But I bet he didn't expect that foam spray from Samson. Oh well! Now old Drac is stuck in the middle of gear bug territory. This ain't gonna be pretty, folks! Yowzah!

I.

Drac Dunwich sat back down in his seat, threw his gun down on the floor of the car, and let out a string of expletives in a high, squeaky voice.

Where the hell did all that foam come from? That was a dirty trick. Drac would have respected Samson a lot more if he had shot knives out of his back fender, or at least pulled out a machete. Drac had been so close to getting his tentacles into Samson's gas tank. Once those things latched on it was impossible for a car to get away without losing the tank in the process.

Now Drac was driving nearly blind through a field, wiping the foam out of his eyes and trying to avoid the random piles of metal junk that littered the Gears.

That's when he hit a wall.

Drac found himself in an old barn. It was set up like a machine shop except where tools would have been hanging on the walls, rotting human body parts hung instead. Most people would have found it revolting but it didn't faze Drac. It made sense for the gear bugs to keep extra parts around. He knew it wasn't about gore or sadism. It was about survival. They were practically falling apart because of the radiation and forced to find ways to compensate. Who was he to judge?

Drac stepped out of his car and surveyed the damage. Other than being covered in a layer of soft white foam, the vehicle was okay. Tentacles slithered around his feet.

He patted the hood. "I know you're hungry," Drac said. "But you'll just have to wait. That Samson is a tricky one. It'll be satisfying to taste him....."

The tentacles retracted.

Footsteps echoed behind him, then all around. Within seconds there were a dozen gear bugs surrounding him, some hanging off the rafters, others emerging from the shadows. Their metal teeth chattered.

Drac's voice squeaked. "You little shits! Do what you came to do, already!"

They were on him at once, swinging their metal limbs and fleshy weapons.

But as quickly as they came, they retreated.

The tentacle hoses shot out from under the car, throwing gear bugs in every direction, and attacked. One tentacle wrapped around a gear bug, squeezing him until his body burst, covering Drac in metallic gore.

Another tentacle went straight through the torso of an ugly hunchback with a fleshy gas tank for a head. Soon all the gear bugs were still, dead and dismembered on the barn floor. Drac stood by, nodding his head and rubbing his glass skull.

"You little shits should have stayed away. I wasn't going to bother you."

He felt a little regret at the massacre but knew it had been inevitable. It was no use reasoning with them. They attacked at the smallest provocation. At least the tentacles got some exercise. Something on the other side of the barn attracted his eye. On a shelf was a pile of vile-looking texts. He picked up the largest book in the pile. The words *Eidolik Podalik* were scrawled on the front in spidery letters. The books were bound with scalps, sheet metal, and rusted gears. The titles seemed to be written in greasy black blood and most were in a language Drac didn't recognize. Drac flipped through the book in his hand catching glimpses of vulgar diagrams of biomechanical incantations: human bodies acting as conduits for infernal fuel. Pornographic pictures of gear bugs were drawn in the margins. Drac threw the book down.

"Now we get going," he said, wiping some foam from under his chin. "Now we get going and win this race."

II.

One Year Ago

Drac sat at his father's ornate wooden table, sipping gasoline.

His father had been dead for three years, bed-ridden for seven before that. While stationed in Afghanistan as a United

States Marine, Drac's father had been paralyzed by the explosion of a roadside bomb. He had managed to get back to the states just before the nukes hit.

It would be humorous if it wasn't so tragic. For years his father had talked about the nuclear weapons the United States had stockpiled and how they could end humanity in one blinding flash. Then he'd ramble on about the Asian countries with biological weapons that could jumpstart a new grotesque evolution full of blasphemous species out of the forbidden abyss of science.

Drac had just nodded. He never believed a war would get to that point. Sure there may be some political posturing and small battles but another world war? It seemed impossible.

But when it happened, Drac was a believer. For all of his father's raving, the man had been right about world affairs.

Drac finished his drink and looked out the window. The scavengers were out there again. They seemed to come in waves, old scholars looking for his father's books. Ten years after the world went to shit, people still looked for knowledge in the printed word. Drac understood. Some people would find it absurd, but he understood too well.

He tapped his glass skull. The sound of gasoline sloshing around inside was comforting.

There was the sound of a car outside. He saw a limousine pull up and a man in a white suit stepped out, chatted with the old scavengers for a minute, and approached the house. Drac grabbed his gun and went to the door.

"Who the hell are you and what do you want?" he said, pulling the door open and shoving the gun in the guy's face.

"My name is Enzo. I represent Mr. Silver."

Drac squinted. He had raced in some of Silver's races before but had never had any personal contact with him. He said, "So?"

"So…Mr. Silver has come to respect your racing prowess and would like to invite you to participate in a special race for him."

Drac put the gun down. "Oh yeah?"

"Yes. Now, may I come in?"

"Okay," Drac said, letting the man in.

They sat in the living room as Enzo laid out the details of the race: the starting point, the rules, and the prizes. Finally Enzo stood up and walked towards the door. "I thank you for your time, Mr. Dunwich and I will tell Mr. Silver the good news. This is gonna be one hell of a race, my friend. Yowzah!"

"Give my regards to your boss."

"I will," Enzo said. He opened the door and then stopped. "Oh, one more thing. Mr. Silver had heard of your father's extensive collection. He wanted me to ask you if you had a certain book."

"Oh?"

"Do you have the *Abgrund Abschaum*?"

"The…..*Abrund Abschaum*…..?"

"Yes."

Drac turned to look at the bookshelf in the living room knowing full well the rare books weren't kept there. They were stored in the downstairs bunker. "I don't remember seeing that one….."

"Oh, that's a shame."

"But if I see it, I'll let you know."

"On behalf of Mr. Silver I'd appreciate that very much."

Drac nodded and shut the door behind Enzo. Visions of starry engines pulsated through his glass skull.

He was ready for the race.

CHAPTER NINE

Yowzah!

What a race, folks! Did you see Drac and his car swat all those gear bugs? I bet those little shits weren't expecting that when they woke up this morning. In fact, I was watching some of the footage from the set-up of the race and I recall seeing some of those gear bugs doing something mighty strange in that barn...something with oil can puppets and colored candles. Weird shit!

And now the racers are making their way into Hoghead Heaven. Let's all say a prayer for them....They're gonna need it!

I.

Samson looked at the sign that read HOGHEAD HEAVEN and thought about Jesus.

He'd never been a religious guy, even before the nukes. It wasn't that he was against having beliefs but he found the idea of faith daunting. Believing in shit you couldn't see, let alone understand, was scary. Before the war, Samson had only believed in people: in their actions and their words. You could keep track of those things. They could be measured, evaluated, proven. It was simple because there was no faith involved. Faith was for the foolish.

Driving into Hoghead Heaven made him think of people who still held on to their beliefs even after the world was practically devastated. Of course, all the destruction and chaos had transformed the religions, making them unrecognizable. There were hundreds of new religious sects, each weirder than the next. Shaved-head Jews that worshipped pig gods. Christians who believed in a pantheon of serial murderers all supposedly related to the Lord Jesus Christ. Buddha-obsessed vegans who venerated (and copulated with) mutated menageries.

Hoghead Heaven was the home of a Christian cult led by Hoghead Slim. There were a lot of strange stories about them, stories involving fungi-fueled visions, mephitic maniacs, and dozens of missing children.

There was no sign of Drac in Samson's rearview mirror, but he did see Junko and Mama Hell come off a side street, yards behind. Junko's Honda looked busted up but the little thing was still zooming alongside the minivan.

There was gunfire as Mama Hell stuck her hand out her window to fire shots at Junko, who swerved to avoid them.

Then Gabby came zooming up beside Samson.

"Jesus Christ," he said. That girl came out of nowhere.

She honked her horn. When Samson looked over he saw Gabby holding her cell phone up to her ear while she steered with her right elbow. Her left hand was busy giving Samson the finger.

"Bitch," he said. There was no time to deal with that brat. Samson maneuvered away from her, moving fast down a street that was becoming gradually more urban than the zone he had just driven out of. He sped by dilapidated buildings separated by grassy trash-filled lots. Telephone poles had been broken and reconstructed into abstract shapes. Unintelligible messages were spray painted on building walls and filthy windows. The street ahead was littered with supermarket carts. Samson slowed down and maneuvered around them.

Then he saw the boy.

The kid couldn't have been more than ten years old. He was running down the sidewalk when he fell in front of an abandoned bicycle shop. Samson slowed down as Gabby zoomed past in the direction of the kid.

"Holy shit," Samson said. That bitch was going to run the kid over. He pulled a lever under the dashboard and a metal tube jutted out from the hood of his car. A grappling hook shot out, digging right into Gabby's trunk. Samson yanked on the lever and the rope went taut. Gabby's car skidded away from the kid. With the push of a button, Samson released the rope from his car, letting Gabby skid out and crash into a mailbox.

Samson drove up onto the sidewalk just past the boy. He opened the passenger's side door. "Get in!" he yelled.

In his rearview mirror he could see Junko and Mama Hell coming up fast. Seconds after the kid jumped into Samson's car, Junko's car crashed into the bicycle shop. Mama Hell's van skidded off into a ditch in front of a tattoo parlor.

"You're lucky, kid," Samson said, putting his car in gear and speeding away.

The boy nodded and rubbed his eyes.

"Are you okay? You hurt?"

The boy touched his elbows. "I'm still awake."

"Yeah. This isn't a dream. You okay?" Samson said. "What's your name?"

"Paulo."

"Samson." He put his hand out and the boy shook it weakly and reluctantly.

There was a few minutes of silence until Paulo said, "The Christians were going to eat me."

Samson said, "What?"

"Hoghead Slim and his Christians. They were going to cook me, they said."

"That's who you were running away from?"

Paulo nodded.

"Jesus Christ, kid," Samson said. "Do you have parents?" He immediately regretted asking that question.

Paulo shook his head. "No."

"Sorry. I didn't mean to…."

The boy shrugged.

Samson stared straight ahead, not wanting to see if Paulo was crying or not. Then he saw them.

The Christians.

They were lined up outside of a building dressed like they were going to a wedding, except they were armed with semi-automatic machines guns and makeshift blade weapons. Samson thought about them eating Paulo. He thought about the tradition of symbolically eating the flesh and drinking the blood of Christ and how these new Christians have been taking that literally. "Close your eyes, Paulo." Samson couldn't resist. He sped up, swerved, and drove through the crowd of cannibals.

A few of them flew onto the hood and over the roof while some went under the tires, their bones crunching along with their weapons. Samson turned on the windshield wipers to clean off the blood.

In his rearview he saw Gabby following, running over the

remaining Christians.

"Hold on, kid," Samson said. "We're getting out of here."

II.

Seven Years Ago

Samson nudged his wife. "Look at him sleeping. He's so cute."

His wife Carol turned her head and saw their son Jack in the backseat, snoring softly. She smiled, "Adorable."

"When we stop, I'm going to work on the car with him. He had some ideas."

Carol said, "I'm not sure I want him helping you, you know, make weapons. You want our little boy doing that kind of stuff?"

"Look around you, hon. The world's changed. Everyone has weapons on their cars now."

"Not everyone," Carol said, looking out the window at the barren wasteland of what used to be eastern Pennsylvania. "Some people have set up peaceful colonies, you know. They only have weapons for emergencies. You have a gun. Isn't that enough?"

"What the hell do you think I need it for? We're not hunting, for Christ's sake, we need them to protect ourselves."

"Still, I don't think I want Jack doing it with you."

"The kid's smart. He likes to be creative and think of things to help his dad. Is that so wrong?"

"Don't make this about him helping you. This is all about macho shit and you know it."

"Whatever, Carol, I'm letting the kid do whatever he wants to do. When he wakes up, you ask him if he either wants to help me arm the car or help you think of names for your peaceful little colony."

"Real cute, Sam. Real cute," Carol said. She looked at him and shook her head. Their arguments usually ended like that, with his being a wise ass and with her staring at him disapprovingly. It was a good thing Jack was asleep. She hated when her son saw them fighting.

"Mommy, where are we?" Jack said from the back seat. He sat up and rubbed his eyes.

"Go back to sleep, sweetie," Carol said.

"No, I want to help Dad with the car."

"Just go to sleep, Jack." Carol gave her husband a look that told him he'd better not undermine her. He ignored it.

"It's okay. You can help, bud," Samson said. He drove a few more miles until he came to a clearing and then he parked the car.

Carol sat on a tree stump reading a moldy issue of *Good Housekeeping* while father and son worked on the car.

"Hey Dad, I had this idea."

"Oh yeah?"

"I thought about, like if someone's following us and we don't know who they are and we want to get away maybe we can have something spray out of the back of the car."

"Like what?"

"What about….," Jack said. "What about that stuff that comes out of fire extinguishers? Like foam or something?"

"Hmm…..You might be on to something, buddy." Samson smiled and patted his son on the shoulder. "We'll see what we can do. We'll have to look around for some supplies the next time we get to a town."

They got back on the road without having done any major

work on the car. Samson thought about how he'd work on Jack's idea for a foam sprayer. While he was drawing the blueprints in his head, he heard the roar of motorcycles behind his car.

"Shit," he said.

"Bikers," Carol said. "Coming up fast, Sam."

"It'll be alright." Samson didn't know if he believed that himself. Most of the bikers on the road were just other people trying to survive. Others, however, just wanted to harass and steal. He had a gut feeling the bikers behind him were of that kind.

There were five of them. They were wearing torn black leather clothing with patches of advertising pinned to the fronts of their vests: Party City, Western Union, American Cyanamid, Cricket Hill, Ohaus, Krauser's, Baby Phat.

The leading biker wore a helmet spray-painted to look like a tomato. On the front of it were the words TOMATO JOE in thick, black letters. The rest of the biker's long, curly hair blew free in the wind. Their bikes were painted red with blotches of black. Each man had a bullwhip wrapped around his neck.

Tomato Joe pulled up on Samson's side and lifted the visor on his helmet. "Pull over," he mouthed.

"No thanks," Samson said, shaking his head.

Tomato Joe flipped his visor down and sped in front of the car with the other bikers following, circling the car like a merry-go-round.

Jack was staring at the gang, partly scared but also a little bit excited.

"Get down, dude," Samson said. "Don't look at 'em."

"Oh come on, Dad."

"Do it!"

"Okay, okay," Jack said, lying down on the floor of the backseat.

Carol whispered. "What are you going to do?"

"Keep going until we hit somewhere that's populated."

"What if that's not for another fifty miles? Then what?"

"I don't know, Carol. What do you want me to do? Stop and make friends?"

"Maybe they're not dangerous, Sam."

"You want to take that chance?"

"What if we just give them some of our supplies?"

Samson laughed. "And then what? They're going to thank us? You think they'll be satisfied with a couple of cans of green beans? Be serious, Carol."

"I *am* being serious."

Samson said, "You want me to pull over? I'll pull over. Okay?" He slowed the car and motioned to the bikers that he was going to stop. "You happy?"

The gang hung back and let Samson bring the car over to the side of the road in front of a sign for MILLIE'S BBQ: *Meet our Finger Lickin' Bar-B-Cuties!*

"Just stay calm and don't offer them a thing, okay? Don't say anything at all," Samson said. "Jack, stay down just in case. Put that blanket over you." He got out and walked to the back of the car where the bikers were pulling up.

Tomato Joe was the only one who didn't get off his bike. Instead, he pulled the visor up and stared at Samson. The other men stood in front of their bikes with their arms folded.

"What's up, guys?" Samson said. "You need help?"

The bikers laughed.

Tomato Joe said, "Nah, but I figure *you* do."

Samson tensed up. "How so?"

"Looks like you have a lot of baggage. We might help by taking that woman off your hands," Tomato Joe said. "Maybe the car, too. It looks to me like you're a man who has too much. You don't want to be greedy, do you? You look like a charitable guy."

"I'm fine the way I am," Samson said. He looked into Tomato Joe's eyes, hoping to show him just the right amount of bravado without things tipping over into a challenge. "You don't have to do this. If you want some shit I can probably give you a few cans of food or some water or something..."

One of the other bikers stomped his foot. "What the fuck did Tomato Joe just say? Did he say he wanted food or water, dipshit? Huh?"

Tomato Joe looked back at the angry biker and said, "Calm down, Bowsman. You catch more flies with vinegar than with... what's the word?"

"Honey," Samson said.

"Wow, looks like we have a bright boy. You a bright boy?"

"No."

Tomato Joe squinted. "You're coming on pretty strong aren't you? Calling me honey and everything."

Bowsman said, "Looks like he wants to snuggle with ya, boss."

Every biker laughed except for Tomato Joe. He said, "That right, bright boy? You wanna snuggle with me?"

"Come on, get serious. My wife and I just want to get out of here. Can't you just give us a break?"

"A break? You want a break? Where was my break when Uncle Sam sent me over to Iraq and I got fucking syphilis from a towel-head whore? Tell me that. Where was *my* break?"

Samson said, "Look, man, I don't know about all that. We're just trying to get..."

"Fuck!" Bowsman said. He walked up to Samson and

slapped him in the face. "Tomato's telling you something and you're being an asshole."

The slap was a weak one but it hurt Samson's ego. He hoped Carol hadn't seen it.

Tomato Joe said, "By the look of his car, I'd say he's a fancy rich asshole." He stepped off his bike but didn't take his red helmet off. He walked up to Samson. "You wanna be my friend?"

"No, not really," Samson said.

"Lemme fuck 'em, boss," Bowsman said. "Lemme fuck 'em real good and hard."

"Nah, nah, calm your shit down, Bow. Take a step back."

The horny biker did what he was told and flicked his tongue at Samson.

Tomato Joe said, "Now, my friend, my stranger, my bright boy, let me tell you what I think. I think we both know you're not going to do shit. It doesn't matter what I decide to do to you, your wife, your car. You see, my man there slapped you and what did you do? Nothing. You didn't do a goddamn thing. You just stood there and took it. Now most badass guys on the road would hit back no matter how many guys were around him. It's an instinct. A *manly* instinct. I think it's called machismo or something. You're a man, aren't you?"

Samson said, "Yeah. I'm a man."

"You sure? I mean, really sure? If we checked your pants, would we find a dick or a pussy?"

Samson shook his head. "Look….."

"A dick or a pussy?"

"Man, come on," Samson said.

"A DICK OR A PUSSY?"

Samson said, "A dick, okay, but listen…."

"SHUT UP. Here's the thing. I don't expect every man to be all manly and shit and strut around like a fucking brute. Hell, before I joined the service I used to be a professional dancer."

Samson attempted to hold in a laugh but wasn't entirely successful.

"Yeah, yeah, you can laugh. I was a background dancer in music videos. Mostly hip-hop, that type of shit, you know? What can I say? I liked to dance and I made money doing it. Then I figured I'd join the Marines and kill me some sand jockeys."

Samson said, "Okay, listen, I appreciate your telling me all this but…"

"Shut up!" Tomato Joe slapped him. "What the fuck do you think I'm doing here talking to you? You think I really want to make friends or something? You think I just want to share my fucking life story? No. That's not what I'm doing. Do you want to know why I'm telling you all this shit?"

Samson shrugged and hoped Carol hadn't seen that slap either. He kept his mouth shut.

"I'll tell you why I'm telling you all this shit. You see, when I'm killing you, when you are inches away from leaving this fucking earth, I want you to know who's killing you. It hurts more, you know. If I was just a fucking stranger and I stabbed you, all you'd think about is who I am and what kind of guy I am and shit like that. I could be any thug or scumbag. But…" He slowly walked around the front of Samson's car. "But…if you know some shit about me, some personal shit, well, that makes the pain of dying worse and it makes me feel pretty good, you know. It's almost like my personality is killing you and not just my physical body. I know that doesn't make much sense but…that's it."

Tomato Joe touched his fingers to the hood of the car and purred. He looked at Carol. "She looks a lot better from this angle. It's like I'm imagining she's in the driver's seat or maybe she's driving one of those foreign cars where the driver is on the other side and I'm thinking about if she tried to run me over. I'd love to see that in slow motion. Her face would be hot like she was getting fucked or something." He rubbed his crotch.

Samson wished he'd bought more bullets for his gun when he had the chance but after weeks of no conflict or trouble, he'd dropped his guard.

Tomato Joe walked back to Samson. "So, what's your move, bright boy?"

"What? What do you mean?"

"Pretend we're in a movie or something. You're the hero and I'm the bad guy. What do you do now? Pull a gun on me or something? Say something tough?"

"Look, I'm telling you I don't want any trouble…"

Tomato Joe laughed and for a split second, he was distracted. Samson lunged for him, landing a punch on the biker's chin and then another in his chest.

Though he thought of himself as relatively strong, Samson was devastated to see his attack had little effect.

Tomato Joe seemed sincerely surprised. "Holy shit! This fucking guy. Wow, I'm impressed, tough guy." He punched Samson in the gut and then pushed him down with a fist to the head.

Bowsman ran over. "Shit, the guy went down easy."

"I bet you like that, don't you, Bow?" Tomato Joe laughed. He looked down at Samson who was groaning in the dirt. "You're pretty weak for a guy who's driving with his wife through the Wastelands. You know, if this was a movie, you couldn't be so damn weak. It makes for a very passive hero and no one likes a passive hero."

"Can I go get the cunt?" Bowsman said. "I think the guys are getting bored over there." The other three bikers were still standing with their arms folded, bouncing on the heels of their feet.

"Let's ask our friend here," Tomato Joe said. He looked down at Samson. "My man here wants to know if we can go get your cunt. Is that okay with you? Can we go get your cunt?"

"Leave her alone," Samson said.

"Holy shit! That's exactly what I expected you to say." Tomato Joe slapped his palm down on the hood of the car. "Bow, go get the cunt and feed her to the guys."

Bowsman walked over to the passenger side of the car and tried to open the door but it was locked. Carol screamed. Bowsman punched through the window and dragged her out.

From the backseat, Jack jumped up. "Let go of my mom!"

"Holy shit," Tomato Joe said. "You've been holding out on us, hero."

Jack was grabbing Carol, pulling her back into the car while Bowsman was pulling her out.

Bowsman said, "Let go of her, you little shithead!"

Tomato Joe put his hand out. "Hold on a second, Bow. Let's see what our friend here thinks." He kicked at Samson. "So you have a kid, too? That makes your passivity all the more pathetic."

"Let them go. Take me, my car, whatever. Just let them go," Samson said, getting his strength back despite another kick from Tomato Joe.

"You see, I knew you were going to say that, too. Okay, so this is what's going to happen. I'm going to take your kid. He's worth some money. I'll take him because those rich folks up north who lost their kids in the war like to buy them. They'd give anything for a fresh kid like yours. They could dress him up, play catch with him or whatever. Some psychos like pretending they have their dead kids back. I don't give a shit myself but they pay good money."

"Fuck you, you're not taking him."

"I wasn't making an offer. I'm just *telling* you I'm taking him. That's it," Tomato Joe said. He turned to Bowsman. "Leave the cunt. Take the kid."

CHAPTER TEN

Holy Sidekick, Batman! It looks like our man Samson has picked himself up a little partner. This should make things interesting. Not only that but I think I saw our girl Gabby getting a little pissed off after missing the chance to run the kid over herself.

Oh, and Junko! If you look closely at the video screens you'll see him tearing some more of his hair out, chomping on it like it's a fistful of black licorice. Yowzah!

I.

Junko was impressed by Samson's rescue of the little boy but was pissed he had crashed into the bicycle shop as a result of it.

When was he going to be shown some respect?

He got out of the car and quickly cleaned the rubble off just in time to see Samson run over the Christians. "Good riddance!" Junko said, remembering a run-in he had had with those crazed zealots a few months back. Once the rubble was off his Honda, he sped off after Samson.

It took him a few minutes to catch up because of the all

debris in the street. The Christians had looted the stores and burnt up all the objectionable material that hadn't been destroyed already. There were burnt piles of comic books, cigarettes, toy dinosaurs, candy bars, sneakers, science textbooks, DVDs, action figures, and dictionaries.

Junko did his best not to drive through the garbage. He'd heard the Christians sometimes hid spikes in them and he had no time for a flat tire. The Honda pulled up right behind Samson and honked.

"Want me to scratch your back?" Junko said. He pushed in his steering wheel which triggered five long blades that extended from the front of his car. "I just got my nails done!"

He stepped on the gas and sent those blades into the back of Samson's car, holding his ground while swerving left and right to inflict the most damage. Shards of metal hit Junko's windshield. He giggled. "Feel good? Feel good? Bet it does!"

Samson's car started to leak white foamy liquid as it tried to pull away but Junko kept on it. Right, left, right left. The blades slit open the back of the car like a tin can.

"Banzai, fucker!" Junko screamed, jamming the blades in even more. He pulled the steering wheel and retracted the blades. Grabbing his shotgun from under the passenger seat, he moved up alongside Samson's car. He wanted to look into the motherfucker's eyes before he blew his head off.

Bringing the gun up, he honked his horn, "Eat this!" He pulled the trigger.

BOOM!

Much to Junko's surprise, glass was crashing into *his* car and his face hurt like he'd been stung by a dozen wasps. Through bloodied eyes he saw Samson smiling. Junko leaned over the passenger seat and lifted the shotgun again. Out the window he saw what had shot him: on top of Samson's car was a giant blowgun, retracting back into the car.

The needles embedded in Junko's face sunk into his skin, burning it. He screamed and fired the shotgun, missing Samson's car and hitting the inside of his own car door.

The Honda swerved to the left, went off the road, and skidded through a grassy vacant lot. It struck a brick wall with graffiti that read *THEE FACE OV THEE BLUE C.*

"Fucking fucker!" Junko yelled, slamming his fists down on the steering wheel, his face gushing thick gobs of blood and poison.

"Maybe…just maybe," he said, grabbing one of his blades. Perhaps if he cut his face off the poison would drain out. Yeah, that sounded like a good idea. But before Junko could follow through with his plan, he was being pulled out of his car.

"Lemme go, fuckers!" he yelled while trying to get a look at his kidnappers through the blood in his eyes. They were just a blur of red and black.

A calm voice said, "Go limp, sinner. It'll be best for everyone."

"Fuck you!" Junko never went limp for anyone and to hell if he was going to start now. He punched and kicked but his broken bones wouldn't carry the force he intended.

Finally someone tied his limbs with wet rope and gagged him with a crumpled up newspaper. Again the calm voice spoke, "Do you wish that we turn your sin to bread?"

Junko felt his dress ride up above his waist, his white panties on full display. Then another voice spoke but this one was less calm than the first. "Don't tempt us, freak!"

Junko resisted with weak spasms while he was dragged across broken glass, sharp stones, and asphalt. His body wasn't the only thing that hurt. Junko's pride had taken a beating. There was just no respect left in the world.

His captors dropped him. Someone wiped his eyes with a smelly handkerchief. Junko was looking through the windows of a butcher shop. He saw that the store had been converted into a chapel. Crosses made of rotting meat and peacock feathers lined the walls while bone-candles formed a rectangle in the middle of the room. A pulpit holding a cash register stood at the far end of the store.

Junko tried rolling over but a kick to the ribs stopped him.

"Stop fighting the will of the Lord, sinner!" a voice said. "Here he comes. Kneel before Hoghead Slim."

A chorus of voices repeated, "Hoghead Slim!"

From the sidewalk, Junko watched as the man named Hoghead Slim approached him. He was wearing wet dress shoes made of leather and a white robe splattered with blood. Slim was tall and wide, rolls of fat rippling under the butcher's garb. The sidewalk thumped with his every footstep. The only thing that was clean was his hair which was immaculately styled with animal fat.

"Sinner, sinner, sinner," Hoghead Slim said. "Your painted face and frilly undergarments won't entice me or my congregation."

Junko looked at Hoghead. The man's head was twice as big as a normal one. It looked like someone had placed a pumpkin on the shoulders of a bulbous scarecrow. Through a mouthful of newspaper Junko said, "Fuck you!"

"I don't understand what you're saying but I imagine it's something vulgar. I would expect nothing less from such a crass display of meat." He crouched down next to Junko and poked him with a sausage-like finger, "You'll soon learn how to properly serve the Lord."

Slim's followers grunted in agreement and then shouted, "Feed him to the Peacock!"

"All in due time, my family." He got close to Junko's face, "Your yellow flesh will turn blue. Then you'll understand His true glory." He snapped his fingers at a woman who handed him a bible. Slim opened the tome slowly, licking his lips.

Junko squirmed, not because he was in any more pain but because he hated religious people. The very sight of a bible pissed him off. He wished he could hock up phlegm from his throat, hurl it at the holy book, and wash the lies away.

Hoghead Slim held the bible open and said, "Dear Lord, what can be done to cure rotten meat? What can be done in your name to turn such a putrid earth spider into something worthy of your glory?" He turned a page in his bible, slipped his hand into the book, and pulled out a fistful of tiny razors, each in the shape of a cross.

"Before you're baptized by the Peacock, you must be cleansed," Slim said, taking the handful of razor crosses and rubbing them along the inside of Junko's thighs, moving up to the crotch of his underwear. "Everything must be cleansed, sinner." He grabbed hold of Junko's penis. "Everything."

II.

Samson sped down a side street, trying to lose Gabby. After a few quick, tricky turns he succeeded. He drove down a street covered in destroyed books and as he did so his car started to make a grinding sound.

"Shit," he said, pulling over. "Stay here. I have to check my car. That Junko guy did some real damage."

"Don't go out there!" Paulo said. "They'll get you!"

Samson pulled out his handgun and showed it to the boy. "I have this. Don't worry about it, okay?"

Paulo nodded his head and frowned.

Samson opened the door and looked around. There didn't seem to be anyone in sight. It was quiet, too, which wasn't really a clue as to the danger that could be hiding. His only hope would be that the Christians were preoccupied with the other racers or the people he had run over.

He got out, slipping on the broken books littering the road. He bent down and looked under his car. That's when he heard the shouting.

Luckily it didn't sound close. Samson looked at Paulo and made a gesture for him to stay in the car. He walked down an alley in the direction of the noise. At the end of the alley there was a brown picket fence and he was just able to look over it.

On the next street the Christians were dragging a bloody, nearly naked figure that could only be Junko towards a giant peacock made out of wood, bone, canvas, and car parts. In the center of the peacock was a large opening that held a bathtub.

"Feed him to the Peacock!" voices screamed. "Feed him good! Then he'll see the light!"

Samson watched as Junko was placed inside the bathtub of the peacock's belly. A large man in bloody white clothes held a flaming torch to the tub as the rest of the people started throwing pages of books into it. Soon Junko was covered and the large man set the torch down into the tub.

It was very faint but Samson thought he heard Junko scream. The peacock's plumage started to flutter, causing a whistling sound like someone blowing across the top of a soda bottle. As the bathtub erupted in flames, the Christians rejoiced. One of them stuck a long scythe into the bathtub and pulled out Junko's fiery corpse, waving it around to the cheers of the crowd.

Samson heard a sound behind him. He turned around with his gun pointed and saw Paulo standing behind him.

"What the hell did I tell you? You were supposed to stay in the car!" Samson shouted.

"I-I-I wanted to see...," the boy said.

"You wanted to see? See what? That?" He turned and pointed over his shoulder. "You wanted to see a man get killed?"

He grabbed Paulo and hoisted him up to see over the fence. "That's what you wanted to see? That?" The Christians were now sticking spoons, forks, and straws into the corpse.

Paulo started to cry.

"No, don't cry now. I told you to stay in the goddamn car." Samson put Paulo down and walked back to the car. He shouldn't have let Paulo see that shit but the kid should have known better. "Let's go."

The boy jogged to catch up and then passed Samson to get into the car. His tears were gone but his expression was one of disappointment, both in himself and in Samson.

Samson took another look under the car and saw a femur bone caught on his exhaust pipe. He dislodged the bone, threw it across the street, and got back in the car.

"You yelled at me," Paulo said, matter-of-factly.

"I know."

"I just wanted to see."

"I know. I'm sorry." Samson patted him on the top of his head. "But next time you have to listen to me, okay? I don't care if you want to see something. You stay in the car. If you can't listen to me then I'll tie you up and put you in the backseat for your own good, okay?"

Paulo nodded.

"Let's get going," Samson said, starting the car and speeding off down the street and out of Hoghead Heaven.

III.

Gabby saw that old bastard rounding the corner, the one who reminded her of her father. He rescued that little brat, the one she had really wanted to run over.

Her cell phone "rang" and she put it to her ear. "Hello? Yeah, I'm following that guy I told you about. Sam something. What? I don't know." She stared out through the windshield at the dilapidated buildings and burnt out shells that used to be houses. A smile appeared on her face. It was nice seeing all the destruction. Stupid people and their ugly houses.

Gabby answered the silence on the other end of the phone. "What? No, I'm okay. I almost had him." She nodded her head while pulling at her shirt. "Hey, can I call you back? My bra is killing me."

It had been ten years since she had a really good bra. The one she wore was sweat-stained and covered in holes. Gabby was pretty particular about the kind she wore. There had been a few opportunities when she could have grabbed a few but they were from Walmart. She'd rather be naked than wearing one of their no-name brands.

With one hand still on the steering wheel, Gabby lifted her shirt and bra. She saw a dark red ring around the bottom of her breasts. The filth of the ten-year old bra had taken its toll. "Eww, gross." Flakes of skin fluttered off onto her legs. She pulled off the bra, rolled down the window, and threw the thing out. In the rearview she saw it take off in the wind like some old designer bird. It landed on a pile of destroyed board games.

She sped down side streets randomly, hoping to get behind that bastard. He was probably her only real competition in the race so she wanted to take him out early. It wasn't just to win the race, however. She'd take great pleasure in running him off the road and popping him open like a can of Red Bull.

Gabby was driving past a comic book store when she saw him.

"Here I come, asshole," she said, speeding up behind Samson. She saw the kid looking back at her and wanted to wipe that innocent look off his face with her knife. But she had to get them to stop first.

Gabby rolled the window down and grabbed her pistol. It was a Desert Eagle she had taken from that asshole named Eastman she fucked and killed back in the Western Wastelands. She remembered he had said he was from Europe which explained his funny accent and the fact that he was as hairy as a fucking Sasquatch.

She stuck the pistol out the window and fired three quick shots at Samson's car.

Samson swerved to the right. That gave Gabby the perfect opportunity to pull up alongside him on the left. She lowered the passenger's side window and pointed the pistol at Samson.

"Oh shit." It took only a split second for Gabby to realize she wasn't going to get the shot off. The barrel of Samson's gun was aimed at her. A flash brought pain to Gabby's shoulder. She went off the road and crashed into a house.

CHAPTER ELEVEN

Yowzah! Sorry all you Junko fans. It looks like our little cutie is fodder for the peacock now. Remember, folks, we never said it was going to be pretty! At least that's something for the Christians to eat.

What about Mama Hell? Or better yet, where in the blazes is our glass-skulled sweetheart Drac? He's got to be around here somewhere....

I.

Drac hauled ass out of the Gears, straight into Hoghead Heaven.

He knew about the religious fanatics who populated the area and if he had to kill a few of the Christians, he was fine with that. There was no way he was going to lose any sleep over a few dead Jesus freaks. Their superstitions were crude and primitive, like the games of mentally-challenged children.

As he drove through the city, Drac saw corpses, fire, and debris. It looked like some shit had already gone down. The race was starting to get interesting. He reached a barricade made of street signs and old plywood. Driving straight through it was an option but there was no point in damaging his car any more than necessary. Drac made a quick right and then a left onto a side street. All the buildings on that road were painted blue and decorated with wings made of bones.

"Don't come out here, people," he said. "I'll fucking destroy you all."

As if answering his challenge, a dozen Christians ran out of buildings on both sides of the street. They were about two blocks ahead but Drac could see they were holding weapons.

"You should have stayed inside, people. Now I'm going to have to mow you down," Drac said, speeding up and sending his tentacles out from under the car. It would be nice to let the tentacles grab a Christian or two, shake them up, and squeeze them like fragile bags of blood. He stepped on the gas and pushed the button for his convertible top to go up. There was no need for the blood of Christians to ruin the upholstery.

As he approached them, they were chanting, "Vanus Christus! Vanus Christus!"

The Christians walked in front of his car as it smashed into them. Bones broke and clothing ripped from the force. The car's tentacles grabbed a fiery young man and twirled him about, squeezing and squeezing until the man's abdomen popped open.

"Thirsty, this makes me thirsty," Drac said. He grabbed a tube from the dashboard and sucked down some gasoline, filling his glass skull. "Fill me up, fill me up."

The tentacles were dragging more Christians behind the car. Their screams harmonized with the roar of the engine. It was music to Drac's ears. He looked in the rearview mirror and saw something large looming on the horizon. It wasn't more

Christians. In fact, it didn't even look human.

II.

"Oh, for goodness sake!" Mama Hell said as she finally got her car out of the ditch. She drove around Hoghead Heaven, navigating around the corpses. She passed the barricade and turned right, taking the same route as Junko.

As she drove down a road lined with blue houses, Mama saw something that made her slam on the brakes. "What the hell…?"

Her van slid across the road and hit the curb. She now had a good view of the monstrosity. It was probably four stories tall, a grotesque giant made of trash, bones, books and wire, possessing a giant penis made out of a telephone pole.

A monster.

Then she saw the ropes.

It wasn't a living, breathing monster. It was a giant marionette.

A fucking *puppet*.

"You got to be kidding me!" she said, putting her van in reverse. The giant stomped closer to her, its legs clanging on the street. She could see dozens of Christians on the roofs of the buildings, pulling wires in unison to make the thing move. The Christians seemed to be screaming something. Mama rolled down her windows as she turned her car around.

"Scrutumi Goliath!" the Christians yelled, as they pulled on their ropes to make the gigantic abomination walk down the street. Its penis slowly wobbled.

Mama Hell's van was facing away from the giant now.

When she stepped on the gas, the car would not move. "What the hell?" she said, stepping on it again. She looked in her rearview mirror and saw chains holding her car in place. The chains led to a telephone pole where a group of Christians were holding torches.

"Scrutumi!" they yelled and threw the torches at her car. The marionette behind them marched faster toward Mama Hell. She stepped on the gas but it didn't do any good. The monster was on the car in seconds, its pole-penis lying on the roof.

"Damn you!" Mama screamed, sending the car into reverse. The van slammed into the marionette's foot and it swayed dangerously, leaning over. Its penis fell down in front of her with a thundering phallic boom.

She could see now that the wooden penis was carved with glyphs, horrible and perverse drawings that reminded Mama Hell of her summer volunteering at a homeless shelter. It disgusted her.

The minivan spun around, speeding away from the Christians and their Goliath. When she was half way down the street, she heard an explosion. In the rearview mirror she watched the tip of the giant penis spurt out a cloud of dust, paper, and rocks. The minivan's back window shattered as the ejaculation reached the car. Crumpled pages of pulp novels fell into the car along with rocks painted blue.

"Freaks!" she screamed, ducking down in her seat and swerving to avoid another load from Goliath.

CHAPTER TWELVE

Wham, Bam, thank you, Mama Hell!

That little lady found herself on the receiving end of Goliath's romance. Yowzah! And so what about the other racers? They're entering a new zone! You know what that means, don't you? More fun! More mayhem! But more importantly...more death!

Yes, it isn't called Hell's Fish Market for nothing! Luckily, however, if the racers can make it through Hell's Fish Market, they reach the one and only gas station on the route. There they may gas up, rest, and plan their next move. For those who just joined us, the drivers are not allowed to attack each other when they're at the gas station. It's neutral territory and if anyone disobeys that rule, well, they'll be decapitated on sight by our resident enforcer, Mr. Block.

Let's hope the local citizens of the Fish Market aren't too angry about being woken up from their slumber. They can get pretty grumpy if they have to leave their water coffins too early.

I.

The route from Hoghead Heaven to Hell's Fish Market curved considerably, bringing the racers near the coast. Once in the heart of the zone, the only road still passable to cars ran right alongside the ocean. Everything else had been blocked off by the inhabitants with spikes, barbed wire, concrete blocks, and other debris.

Samson sped down the road, the beach to the left of him and wreckage to the right. He wanted to get to the gas station as soon as possible.

He turned to Paulo who was looking out the window. "Hey kid."

"Yeah?" Paulo said, not taking his eyes off the ocean.

"Did you live in Hoghead Heaven?"

Paulo's chin dropped to his chest while he shook his head.

"Okay."

There were a few more minutes of silence and then Samson said, "You know, I had a family once. But…"

Paulo interrupted him, "They died in the war?"

"No," he said. "I was lucky, my family survived through all that shit. How about you? I know you don't really want to, you know, talk about it. But I mean, it's good to do that, talk about it. It might make you feel better about things."

Paulo shook his head.

"Okay," Samson said. "But I think it's nice that even after the war, your parents had you and took care of you and if it wasn't for those goddamn Christians…"

"What happened to your family?" Paulo said.

"They…well, I had a son…but he's probably dead."

"That's sad."

"I guess deep down I think he's alive, though. You know I really thought after the war, after all that shit, the nukes and everything, that I'd be okay because I had my family. We were doing alright, despite everything around us. Because of my job I knew a lot of people all over the country and we had friends we could connect with if we needed help. I think we were lucky."

"What was the war like?"

"I only know from TV. I wasn't in the war or near any of the bomb sites. But even then it was hell. We first heard about a foreign city getting bombed and then one that was a little bit closer to the USA and then closer and closer. Then a city inside our own country, and then closer and closer again. I think the whole country was shocked we were even hit at all, let alone with nukes. It was crazy. People freaked out all over. Some looted stores, some just holed up in churches, some went around killing people. Some people just sat back and figured it'd all go back to normal, you know? They thought the president would fix everything. But you know where the president was? He was dying of some plague or something from a biological weapon."

"Sounds scary," Paulo said.

"Yeah."

"Where are you going to get food?"

"There should be some stuff at the gas station. But if we win the race, we'll get a lot. That's one of the prizes. Food and gasoline….and a safe place to live."

Paulo frowned. "Someone's just going give that to you if you win?"

"Yeah," Samson said. "At least that's what they said. You never know what someone's going to end up doing."

"We're going to the gas station now?"

"Yeah."

"What kind of food is going to be there? Seafood? Fish and stuff?" He pointed to the ocean.

Samson laughed. "You don't want to eat the seafood around here, kid. It's all radioactive. The people who live near here are all screwed up from it. They don't even sleep in real beds. They sleep in bathtubs filled with ocean water."

"But then where do they get the food?"

"I think they brought the food from somewhere else... or at least I hope so," Samson said. He looked in the rearview mirror. "Oh shit."

It was Drac Dunwich.

"Shit, he's fast." Samson felt like slowing down and getting behind him to mess the guy up but knew that was too much of a risk. Instead, he kept the guy in his sights and waited for Drac to make a move.

A loud pop shook him.

"What was that?" Paulo said.

"It's a goddamn tire." Samson felt the car flutter and swerve to the right. He navigated around a few potholes, pulling into a small alcove made of barbed wire and large concrete chunks. Luckily, Drac sped past him, tentacles waving obscenely to Samson as the car passed.

"Shit," Samson said, grabbing his gun and getting out of the car.

"Wait!" Paulo said, opening his door.

"Stay here. Remember what I said, okay?"

Paulo nodded and got back into his seat.

Samson surveyed the damage. Yes, one of the front tires was flat but he didn't have a spare tire. There was supposed to be shit like that at the gas station but how the hell was he going to get there now?

There was a noise coming from the beach across the street: coughing and the rattle of shells. Samson cocked his weapon and stared in the direction of the sea.

A tall, shirtless man was walking across the beach toward the road, holding a net full of crabs, some alive but some quite obviously dead. Samson thought the man looked harmless, even a little bit friendly. When they made eye contact, the man smiled and waved with his one free hand.

"How's it going?" the man said, looking both ways and crossing the street to Samson and his car.

"Okay," Samson said, still gripping the gun tightly. As the man got closer, Samson could see the crabs in the net were horribly deformed. One resembled a human infant with a dark yellow shell.

The man said. "You in the race?"

"Yeah."

"No need for the gun," the man said. He turned completely around to show Samson that he wasn't hiding a weapon. "I ain't armed."

"Doesn't mean you're not dangerous."

"Good point." The man smiled. "I'm Lee." He dropped the crab net and sat down, putting his palms on the ground beside him. "See? I'll just sit here like this. Then we can talk. I can help with the tire if you want."

"Why so helpful? Not that I don't appreciate it or anything, but it's not something I'm used to." Samson thought the guy might be working for Mr. Silver, put there to help or hinder the drivers. Or he could just be a lone psycho, itching to mess with anyone.

"Man, I'm just a guy who lives off the sea and likes to walk on the beach, do my thing. I don't mean any harm to anyone, even the mean ones, you know, the ones who have lived here their whole lives, the ugly ones, know what I'm saying?"

Samson said, "So you don't live here? In the Fish Market, I mean."

"Nope. I just go up and down the coast. Do what I can to get by," Lee said. "I know where there's some tires. The people here, they don't need tires and cars and things like that. You want help?"

Samson took a quick look in the car and saw Paulo staring at him. It was risky having a stranger assist him with the car but it might be their only hope for getting the car fixed. One of Mr. Silver's guys might come around eventually but that could take hours. If he kept the gun ready at all times, letting this guy Lee help them out might not be a bad idea.

He said, "Sure, that'd be great. Thanks."

"May I stand up?"

"Yeah."

Lee stood up and walked back to the beach. "Be right back," he said over his shoulder. Samson kept his gun ready.

A minute later Lee came back, rolling a tire beside him and smiling widely. "Here it is. Hope it fits."

"Thanks," Samson said. "What do I owe you?"

Lee laughed, "Nothing."

"You gave me a tire. I assumed it was a trade."

"No trade. I just found the tire on the beach. Not my tire. I'll even put it on for you if you want. You're in a race, right? Take some time to relax."

"Why the hell are you being so nice? What the hell is your angle, Lee?"

"No angle, man. I told you, I just like to get by. I like to go through my days without any conflicts, any problems. I found out a long time ago the best way to do that is to just be nice."

"You're going to end up getting killed one of these days, you know that?"

Lee smiled. "Yeah, I know it."

Samson let Lee change the tire all the while keeping his gun hand relaxed and ready just in case. As soon as the new tire was on the car, Paulo opened his door slowly and walked out. He stared at Lee.

"How are you, sport?" Lee said.

"Fine." Paulo walked over to Samson.

Lee said, "So what's your story? This your dad?"

Samson interrupted. "No, I'm not. I found the kid in Hoghead Heaven. The Christians were chasing him."

"Those goddamn Christians always killing kids and pregnant women. Shit, those are some crazy people."

"They do that a lot?"

"Yeah. You don't know that part? They want to cleanse the earth or something and so they think people shouldn't populate it anymore. If they see a pregnant woman, they kill her. They don't care. Shit, they worry about humans killing the earth and all that but they kill kids, man. They eat people and all that. Won't eat a crab or anything but they'll chop into a person and cook them right up." Lee saw Paulo was getting upset. "Sorry, sport. I shouldn't be talking about this stuff."

Paulo looked down and said, "Are you part of the race?"

"Me? No. Thank god for that."

Samson said, "What'd you hear about it?"

"All I know is that this is supposed to be the race to end all races. Death, destruction, and all that shit."

Samson said, "Thanks again, Lee."

"No problem. Oh, take some crabs, too. Not the best tasting but they're good when you're hungry." He handed Samson one of the more normal looking crabs in the net. "Just cook it real good and it'll be fine."

Samson took the animal graciously, although he had no intention of eating it. Out of the corner of his eye he could see Paulo looking at the crab in confusion.

The men shook hands. Samson and Paulo got into the car together and they drove away, watching Lee wave to them in the rearview mirror.

"We're not going to eat that crab, are we?" Paulo said.

Samson laughed.

The man named Lee watched the car as they drove away, giggling to himself.

II.

Seven Years Ago

Tomato Joe laughed.

He revved the engine of his bike and laughed. Samson watched his son grow smaller down the road, tied to the back of Tomato Joe's motorcycle. The boy was nothing now but a piece of merchandise.

Samson lay on the ground next to his car, crying hysterically. He had failed as a father. He had fought when the bikers had grabbed Jack. He had even landed a good punch right on Bowsman's jaw. But it was too late. He was outnumbered. They pummeled him with fists, feet, and whips. They urinated on him.

Carol tried desperately to prevent Jack's abduction but she was slapped to the ground and raped by Tomato Joe's men. She was bruised and violated while Samson was held down by

Bowsman, forced to watch.

When the bikers left, Samson was able to look Carol in the eyes though he didn't really want to. There was nothing there but hate. She wished they had taken *him* instead of Jack.

He said, "I'm sorry."

Carol face's exploded into a grotesque rage. Samson had never seen her so ugly. Her words bombarded his ears but he couldn't wrap his head around what she was saying. It was the explosion of everything she had ever disliked about her husband and the father of her only child. It was a mother's wrath from a damaged mind.

After a barrage of curses, Carol picked up a large rock and slammed it down on Samson's head, knocking him out. When he awoke, the car was gone and so was his wife.

CHAPTER THIRTEEN

Yowzah! This is exciting, folks! Our racers are nearing the service station. It's time for them to fill their vehicles up, get a few extra supplies and some complimentary refreshments. Boy, do they need it! Yowzah!

It looks like our man Samson just got a little roadside assistance from New Jersey's favorite psycho Lee Basatan. Isn't that hilarious?

I.

The gas station was surrounded by bare-chested men in torn denim jeans. They held guns and blades of various types but all wore the same style of dark aviator sunglasses. Their muscles flexed uncontrollably, their pores sweat green pus.

Drac's car was next to the first pump sucking down gasoline through several tentacles while Drac himself was leaning against his vehicle, looking out into the distance to see what had happened to Samson.

He had been tempted to mess with the guy on the side of the road but there was something dishonorable about that. Sure, Drac wanted to win the race. He wanted to win it with every fiber of his freakish being but he still couldn't bring himself to snuff a guy stuck on the side of the road with a flat tire.

Drac walked over to another pump, pulled a hose off, and put the nozzle to his mouth. As he sucked down the gasoline, his transparent head filled with amber liquid. He felt stronger, more focused, more intent on winning the race.

"Hey, dumbass," said a voice behind him. He turned around to see the woman who dressed like a teenage girl and talked into her cell phone like a crazy person. Gabby.

"What?" Drac said.

Gabby laughed. "What the hell is wrong with your voice? You sound like a little girl."

"What do you want?"

"Stop hogging the gas, dipshit." She started playing with her hair, putting it into a ponytail, taking it out of the ponytail, putting it back in a ponytail. "Leave some for the rest of us."

"You want to start something, do it on the road. Then you'll see," Drac said, nodding his head and pointing at the road.

Gabby laughed. "Yeah, I bet I will, fag." She walked away toward the main building of the gas station. Several guards were standing around, eyeing the racers and smoking mushroom cigarettes. She walked up to the biggest guard and said, "Hey, you mind if I...?"

The guard puffed pinkish smoke into the air and held out the cigarette to Gabby. She took it and helped herself to a long deep drag. "Thanks." She gave it back to the man and walked away.

The drug hit her like a sloppy fist. Yellow hues shoved a headache into her skull, twisting her neck around until she was looking out at an obscure angle. Everyone around her wore thin veils over their faces: some yellow, some green, some red. Black, bulbous forms appeared in the sky behind red lights flickering on the horizon. Gabby took a few steps and no longer felt the dirt below her feet but rather cold cobblestones.

Squid-like insects crawled out from in between the stones followed by plump, two-tailed scorpions. Gabby tried stomping them with her foot but they simply crawled up through her tennis shoe. The sound of a toilet flushing reverberated through her skull followed by the sound of a high-pitched cough and the slow, sloppy sounds of bored sex.

"Eww, gross!" she said, falling backwards. The guard who had given her a puff of his cigarette caught her in his burly arms. She saw herself in the reflection of the man's aviator glasses. The bottom half of her face was made of short, pink tentacles.

The man said, "Good stuff, eh?"

The insects faded along with the bulbous, black forms in the sky. Gabby's headache disappeared as she coughed up yellow smoke. "What the fuck did you give me?"

"Just a little bit of the tcho," he said, blowing a kiss.

"Asshole," Gabby said as she watched the man walk away along the building. She wished she could shoot that motherfucker in the head.

A hand fell on Gabby's shoulder. "Don't you worry about him, honey."

Mama Hell was behind her, giving a motherly smile. Gabby scowled and shook the hand from her shoulder. "Excuse me?"

"You know men. They just like playing with a cute girl."

"Why don't you mind your own business, you fat bitch?"

Mama Hell's smile disappeared instantly. Her eyes narrowed and her mouth curled. "You want me to ram my fat fist up your little cunt?"

Gabby stared.

Mama Hell smiled. "I can fondle your womb, honey." She moved her face close to Gabby's. "Don't tempt me."

Gabby walked away, her eyes wide and her jaw trembling.

Mama Hell laughed and turned to watch as Samson finally pulled up to the pumps.

II.

Mama was glad to watch as that handsome son of a bitch pulled up to the pumps. It allowed her to take her mind off the race. There wasn't time to seduce the man. Even if there was, she wouldn't be able to do it without thinking of her late husband and that wasn't something she wanted to do.

Mama watched Samson get out of his car. The guy looked apprehensive, even skittish. It wasn't what she expected to see in someone taking part in Silver's death race. She made eye contact with him and said, "Hey sailor."

Samson nodded.

Mama walked over to the passenger's side of his car and looked through the window at Paulo. "Cute boy. You're a sweetheart for saving him."

Samson shrugged.

"Man of few words, huh?" Mama said. She scrunched up her face in a smile and waved at Paulo who did not return the gesture.

"What do you want?" Samson said.

"No reason to get all bent out of shape, honey. Just trying to be nice. All this violent racing, you'd think people would want some nice conversation to calm their nerves."

"My nerves are fine."

"Wow, you need to loosen up, sweetie." Mama tapped the roof of the car and walked away.

Samson shook his head and went to the pump. He remembered a time when you didn't have to pump your own gas in New Jersey. You would just sit in your car and let the guy do it for you.

A high-pitched voice from across the lot said, "Hey."

Samson looked over and saw a glass skull looking at him from above a gas pump. It was Drac.

"Yeah?"

"You drive well."

"Thanks," Samson said. What the hell was the guy trying to do? Lure him into some sort of fake camaraderie in order to exploit his weaknesses? Not a chance. He cut off eye contact with Drac and then ducked his head into the car to talk to Paulo.

"You okay, bud?"

Paulo was holding onto the crab like it was a teddy bear. "I guess."

"That Mama Hell woman scare you?"

"A little bit."

"Well, she scares me, too," Samson said. He smiled. "But just a little bit."

Paulo giggled and let the crab loose. He crawled over into the driver's seat and said, "You think I can steer a little bit later?"

"I like you, kid, but not that much." He looked over to see if Drac was still looking at him. He wasn't. "You want to come with me to get some food, kid?"

"No, I'll stay here."

"Sure?" Samson said. The boy nodded. "I'll be right back."

He walked to the main building where a few of Silver's vendors were selling everything from dried horseshoe crab to shoe-leather moonshine.

The first vendor Samson reached had a selection of seafood but he had never liked the stuff. The short man who was selling it was wearing a shirt declared him the last of the "Outlaw Order."

"What? You don't enjoy seafood?" the outlaw said.

"No, I don't." Samson walked over to the next person but the outlaw grabbed hold of his arm.

"I got squid, man. Ever had squid? I mean good squid, not that shit you get at Jap restaurants. I'm talking Grade-A squid, man, the best. Mr. Silver has it shipped in from Queensbreath. That's in England, you know."

"No thanks," Samson said, pulling himself out of the outlaw's sharp, dirty nails.

"Suit yourself, asshole," the outlaw said. He started muttering to himself. "Too good for squid, Blue Christ."

The next vendor sold what looked like homemade candy and small jars that were labeled "mixed fruit juice" but were probably just a mixture of water, tree sap, and the tiniest amount of liquid from a real piece of fruit. An unscrupulous vendor could make fifty bottles of "mixed fruit juice" with one orange and a whole lot of toxic rain water.

Still, it would be nice to have something other than water to drink. So he grabbed two bottles of the "fruit juice" and looked up at the vendor.

This guy was a tall man covered in red tattoos. Metal spikes protruded from the sides of his eyes as well as his chin. "Two juices?"

"Yeah."

JORDAN KRALL

"Twenty."

Samson dug into his pockets and paid the man. New Jersey was one of the only places where old pre-war currency was used in addition to trade.

A high-pitched voice behind him said, "The juice is terrible."

Samson turned his head to find Drac Dunwich standing there grinning at him.

"What do you want from me?" Samson said, tensing up, his heart fluttering into flight mode. He didn't have his gun on him.

"Want? Nothing. What do you think I want?"

"Stay away from me, okay? You want a go at me, fine. Save it for the road."

Drac's smile disappeared, replaced by a sickly frown. The gasoline in his glass skull bubbled. "You think? Look at my car. That is pure road hell brutality at its finest. It'll beat you, no contest."

Samson couldn't believe that a guy with a glass skull and a voice like a little girl would talk to him like that. He wanted to hit him in the face with the two jars of juice. "We'll see," he said.

Drac said nothing. He stared straight at Samson as his teeth started to chatter. Samson expected them to pop out of his mouth at any second but before they could, Drac turned around and walked back to his car.

"Jesus Christ," Samson said. He was ready to continue the race. They were just waiting for an announcement from the loudspeakers that hung from the top of the service station.

He walked back to the car, saw his tank was full, and put the hose back. As he was turning back to the car, Mama Hell shrugged out of her sweater at the next gas pump, revealing bare skin beneath.

But it wasn't *her* skin.

Draped over her shoulders was a shawl of flesh covered in red tattoos and glistening with sweat. Two holes were cut out of the front to let Mama's heavy, drooping breasts out where they hung, their areolas staring sinisterly like the pancake-sized eyes of an evil squid.

Samson couldn't tear his eyes away from her chest as the tattoos on her flesh-vest moved into obscure and complex shapes, circling around each areola like a crimson whirlpool. A bitchy voice broke his trance.

"Ew, gross, put a shirt on!" Gabby yelled at Mama Hell who responded with a smile and a middle finger.

A loud voice echoed out from loudspeakers, "Yowzah! Racers, it's Enzo here. Finish your business and get ready to roll! In ten minutes the race will continue and it'll be no holds barred and, yowzah, wait a second.....we have a special announcement by Mr. Silver himself!"

Everyone at the service station stopped what they were doing and perked their ears to listen closely.

"Greetings, my dear drivers, my dead road killers," Mr. Silver said. "I have some special news for you all, something I hope will make the race much more exciting. As you know, after you leave the service station you'll be heading into the Zone of Dead Roads. What you may *not* know is that the zone is inhabited by both the Yuggs and the Zoners. I am here to offer an extra challenge as the race continues. Find the leader of the Zoners, he is called Lord Bing Bong, and *kill* him. His people have made it difficult for the Yuggs and I do have a soft spot for those ugly little things. So there it is. The one to kill

Lord Bing Bong gets a special prize. Now get ready. The race will continue in seven minutes."

Samson felt a tug on his shirt. It was Paulo.

"What's a Yugg?"

"Not sure. Never saw one but I think they're some kind of typical post-nuke freak, a mutant."

Paulo nodded. "I have to go to the bathroom," he said.

"You should've gone earlier, kid. We gotta get going."

"I'll be quick."

Samson put his hand on Paulo's back and guided him as they followed the signs to the restroom on the side of the service station. The door was covered in yellowed newspaper headlines all exclaiming events leading to the nuclear holocaust of 2015.

The bathroom consisted of one dirty sink and a dirtier toilet. Gas station bathrooms were never clean to begin with but this one was disgusting. The floor was invisible beneath feces, hair, papers, and other unidentifiable debris. "Don't touch anything," Samson said. "Just unzip, piss, and we'll get out of here. Don't even touch the sink to wash your hands, okay?"

Paulo nodded and walked to the toilet. While he urinated, Samson looked outside to make sure no one was coming up to take them by surprise. When the boy was done, Samson glanced back inside. Paulo was staring at the mirror.

"Look," he said.

"What?" Samson said. His eyes went to the glass where he saw words written in the grease:

That is not dead which can eternal lie,
And with strange engines even death may drive.

"What's that mean?" Paulo said.

"I don't know. Let's go." Samson grabbed Paulo by the shirt and walked him out of the restroom. As they approached the car, Drac stared at them, his gasoline-filled skull reflecting the sun, spreading bars of bright light in all directions. For a moment it looked like Drac's head was on fire. A cloud moved in front of the sun and the bars of light dissipated.

No such luck.

It was time to get rolling. Samson closed the door of the car and started the engine. The sound put him at ease. Despite the bad memories, being on the road provided Samson with a way out of his head. He sensed there might be more horrible things to come even if, by some chance, he did end up winning the race.

The sense of dread and impending danger reminded Samson of a dream he'd had several weeks ago. It wasn't unusual to have vivid, violent dreams after the war. Some said the nuclear fallout and biological contaminants affected the brain in ways no one quite understood. But this dream had felt different than any other.

He stood under a waterfall. Someone was with him. At first he thought it was Carol, and then Jack before he realized it was neither. The force of the water kept him paralyzed for what seemed like hours until something slithered up his leg and wrapped around his waist. An intense heat filled his bowels and the person next to him whispered in his ear.

"We're here for a reason. We were here from the beginning."

The waterfall trickled to nothing and Samson found himself standing in a parking lot surrounded by gas pumps. The person was still next to him but every time Samson turned to look at them, they scooted into his shadowy, peripheral vision. All at once the pumps started to rumble and then shoot off into the air. From underneath the earth came a deluge of yellow sludge and again Samson found himself paralyzed.

The yellow sludge got closer and closer until finally, Samson woke up.

"We're here for a reason. We were here from the beginning."

CHAPTER FOURTEEN

Yowzah! The drivers have refueled and now it's off into the Zone of Dead Roads.

For those who missed it, Mr. Silver himself has given our contestants another challenge: kill Lord Bing Bong and earn a bonus! Let's see if our racers will take advantage of it. For the sake of pure unadulterated entertainment... I sure hope so!

I.

One Year Ago

Gabby loved racing.

But what she loved even more than racing was winning. She believed whole-heartedly that she deserved to win each and every race she entered and she usually did.

But she'd been having dreams for three nights straight.

Bad dreams.

At first she was floating high above the earth, slowly and peacefully, unknown celestial bodies coming into view and disappearing. Then her body would drop to the earth, into the deep blue of the sea. She would start to swim, moving through the water like a great white shark, swerving left and right to find her prey.

She knew instinctively that she was a predator, knew that she was hunting for the most perfect and delectable prey.

But something would grab her body. It happened every time, in every dream, every night. It happened the same way. At first she thought her body had been caught in seaweed, but the slimy ropes were moving. Alive. Then she would realize they weren't ropes. They were tentacles. At first, there were a few, but they multiplied quickly until her whole body was covered in them. The suckers glued to her flesh, pulsating with furious hunger.

Then there came a sharp pain between her legs.

And that's when she would awake...sweaty, scared, and bleeding from the crotch.

As she woke, the terror of the dream would fade. After an hour, Gabby forgot about the dream completely.

That afternoon, she was detailing her car when someone tapped her on the shoulder.

It scared the shit out of Gabby and she grabbed her gun, pointing it at the person behind her. When she saw who it was, she put the weapon down.

"Enzo," she said.

"At your service, young lady."

"So is Mr. Silver letting me in the race or what?"

Enzo put his finger to his chin and cocked his head. "Well..."

Gabby grabbed the man's collar. "I want in, dickhead."

"I'm just fooling with you, sweetie. Of course you're in. Mr. Silver would be happy to have you."

"Good."

Enzo explained to Gabby the details of the race but she only half-listened. Instead, she was thinking about how many people she'd get to kill on the road.

When Enzo left, Gabby felt extremely tired despite it being early in the afternoon. She got into her car, leaned the seat back, and fell asleep.

She had another dream.

This time, she did not wake when the pain struck between her legs. The dream went on, the tentacles squeezed and the suckers bit into her flesh, vibrating until finally she was ripped into pieces from the inside.

Then she woke up.

She was relieved it was only a dream. It didn't matter what had happened there in her sleep. Dreams were just fantasies of the mind.

Dreams never came true.

II.

When the horn sounded, Drac sped out of the gas station and onto the road, taking a small turn off to the right of the main highway. When he was a half mile ahead of the other drivers, he saw what looked like a speed bump in the road. But it couldn't have been a speed bump.

It was moving.

As he was driving up on it, Drac saw it was a parade of crabs of all shapes, sizes, and colors. He could hear the clicking of their claws over the sound of his engine. The crunching sensation beneath his tires brought his mind back to the race. In his rearview mirror he saw that little bitch Gabby coming up fast. "You want to pass me? Go ahead and pass me," he said, slowing down.

Gabby didn't waste any time in speeding up alongside the passenger's side of Drac's car, shooting her gun wildly.

Drac slowed down, moved to the right, and rammed Gabby's car while his tentacles slid underneath to puncture her gas tank.

The bitch swerved over and yelled, "Fucking freak!"

Five seconds later she was skidding off the road, her car's gas tank quickly being siphoned while another tentacle was forcing itself into the engine. Drac decided he wasn't going to waste any time getting that bitch out of the race even if it meant not being able to take a shot at Lord Bing Bong.

Gabby's vehicle spun three-hundred and sixty degrees, her car torn apart by Drac's tentacles. She was screaming with rage as she realized the race was over for her unless she got another car.

Drac's car.

She jumped out of her mutilated car, guns blazing, shrieking like a banshee. Her blonde hair was flapping angrily in the wind. Gabby wasn't aiming her guns but she came pretty close to hitting Drac.

"You got balls, bitch," Drac said, trying to retract the tentacles from the wreckage of Gabby's car. He'd have to handle her the old-fashioned way. No big deal. He had no qualms with fighting a woman face to face. Besides, that bitch wasn't much of a woman. She was just a typical delusional head case of the post-apocalyptic world.

III.

Who the hell did that glass-skulled freak think he was?

Gabby had been talking to her friend on the phone when that piece of shit sent his tentacles under her car. "I'll have to call you back," she said, putting the phone down and holding on as her car spun around.

When she realized her car was totaled, she jumped out and started shooting like a crazed gunslinger. She didn't have the patience aim at the motherfucker. It was just: blam-blam-blam.

Gabby thought about the dozens of people she killed in the last ten years. Each one had been more satisfying than the last. Snuffing out this freak would be the best kill ever.

IV.

Drac got out of the car and stood with his gun at his side, assessing the crazed woman in front of him. He wondered what impression he made on her with his glass skull full of gasoline, spiked shoulder pads, and inhumanly bulging muscles. Image was important in the wasteland. First impressions were what either struck fear into someone's mind or made them think of you as an easy target.

Spittle flew from Gabby's mouth as she shrieked at him. The car's tentacles whipped out of Gabby's car. It took only a few seconds for them to find their target.

One tentacle wrapped around Gabby's upper body and lifted her off the ground while another would its way up between her legs. A third entered her mouth. Her eyes bulged and so did her stomach. The bitchy look was still on her face. Drac figured it was probably something she couldn't get rid of, even in death.

Drac could never get used to that sound. It was something between the crinkling of paper and the slapping sounds of sex. Though they were his tentacles and were under his control, this time they didn't seem to be following his directions. Drac would have never sent one of the tendrils in between her legs, though there he was staring at one of them inching its way up there slowly for maximum pain. Finally it pulled out and showered the ground with Gabby's insides. Her organs landed in the toxic moss.

Drac got back in the car and revved his engine. He thought it sounded like that dead bitch's screams.

V.

"Where are we going?" Paulo asked.

"Gonna see a friend of mine," Samson said. "He might be able to take care of you." Though he thought about killing Lord Bing Bong, he knew it would be smart to visit his friend Cobra Canfield first and drop the kid off. The guy had been living in the Zone of Dead Roads for as long as Samson could remember and he was the only person there that could be trusted. Also, he had a constant supply of weaponry.

"Who?" the boy said.

"Just a friend."

"I don't want to stay with him. I want to stay with you."

"It's not up for discussion, kid. I can't take you along. It's too dangerous."

The car veered off to the right in a cloud of dust. Two miles later they were navigating around boulders painted a deep red.

"We're almost there," Samson said, looking carefully at the boulders until he saw the one he was looking for. There was a tiny flash of blue light. He pulled the car around the back of that boulder and turned off the engine. "Here we are."

Samson got out of the car and motioned for Paulo to follow. The boy was reluctant to get out in the middle of nowhere. Samson put his arm around the boy's shoulder and told him it was going to be okay.

A small door opened up in the boulder revealing a tall black man with a Fu-Manchu mustache. He wore a purple t-shirt with the word WRENCH scrawled in black across the front. The man said, "Well holy shit, if it isn't the man himself. Je-sus Christ, good to see you, Samson."

"Cobra." The two men hugged briefly and Cobra extended his hand for Paulo to shake.

"How you doing, little man?"

"Good, sir."

Cobra laughed. "No need to call me sir. Makes me feel old." He looked at Samson. "Saw you guys coming from a mile away. Was gonna take a shot at you just for fun, you know, keep you on your toes."

"Then I would've had to kick your ass."

"Or at least you'd try," Cobra said, laughing. "Is this a friendly visit or you need something? And who's this little man?"

"This is Paulo. Found him during the race…"

Cobra interrupted. "Race? Jesus Christ, Samson, you doing that shit?"

"Yeah, yeah, I know. I don't need you to talk me out of it."

"Well, I won't. I assume it's too late anyway."

"I came by to see if you could do me a favor."

"Sure thing."

"It's kind of a big one."

Cobra cocked his eyebrow. "Spill it, Samson."

"I need you to take care of this kid."

Cobra rolled his eyes. "Come on, man. You seriously gonna ask me for a favor like that? This ain't no place for a kid." He looked at Paulo. "Nothing against you, little man. Just take a look around and you see what I'm saying."

Samson said, "Look, you have connections and I'm sure you can find someone to take care of him, some nice family or something. Just watch him until the end of the race and if I… survive, I'll come back and get him. Okay?"

"Shit, man," Cobra said. He put his hands on his hips and shook his head. "Jesus Christ. Okay, fine."

"Thanks. Now for my second favor. You have any weapons? Specifically blow gun refills."

Cobra shook his head. "You're pushing you luck, brother." He laughed and motioned for them to follow him. "Let's go inside and talk." He led them through the door in the boulder, up a staircase to a small loft. There was a table set up with an old teapot and various dried meats, some brown and others dark green. Cobra motioned around the room. "This here's one of the rocks I go to when I just want to, you know, relax."

"We can't stay long."

"If you want your stuff…sit down."

The three of them took a seat while Cobra poured them some hot meat-water. He opened up a cabinet in the wall and took out crates of weapons. "I'm low on new weapons. Haven't had my person come by in quite a while. I do have your blow gun darts and some bullets, though."

Samson took the supplies and said, "What do you know about the race?"

"Shit, what do *you* know about the race? I know you've raced before but that was for, what, food and gasoline? Canadian dollars? What the hell is Silver offering the winner?"

"Food, gasoline, supplies. A job."

"A job? Working for him? Christ, Samson, you gotta be smarter than that."

"What the hell else am I supposed to do?"

"There's something else, isn't there?"

Samson shook his head. "I don't know what you're talking about."

"And what about the kid? How'd he get wrapped up in this?"

"Saved his life during the race so I took him along."

Cobra sighed. "And now you're on your way to win this race?"

"Yeah."

"Well, good luck to you even if you are a stupid son of a bitch."

Samson chuckled. "Hey, another thing. Silver wants the racers to kill a guy named Lord Bing Bong. You know him?"

Cobra said, "Shit, man, you serious?"

"Yeah, why?"

"That dude is bat-shit crazy, man. Dangerous, too. Silver probably figures most of you ain't gonna survive trying to bring Bing Bong down."

"Well, I didn't say I was going to try for it. The time I spent here already means I'm going to be behind. I figured those other assholes will be preoccupied with him. Might give me a better chance."

"You think you're the only racer to have that idea? I'd get going if I were you," Cobra said. "And speaking of which…I'm glad as hell I ain't you. No offense."

Samson grunted. "Yeah."

Cobra turned to Paulo. "Looks like you're staying with Uncle Cobra. Can't say I have much in the way of toys but I have a dirt bike I'm almost done fixing. You might like to take a ride on that when it's done. How about it?"

Paulo said, "What's a dirt bike?"

The men laughed. They shook hands and went outside.

"I owe you," Samson said.

"You get out of that shit alive and we meet again, you can pay me back in good conversation and a game of chess."

"I'm sure I'll find time to kick your ass."

Cobra laughed.

Samson went into the backseat of the car and pulled out the crab he had gotten from Lee. "You have any use for this?"

Cobra smiled. "Sure do."

"You might be able to trade it to someone. You can't eat it, though. It's not safe."

"Sure as hell I can. My stomach's made of iron." Cobra took a huge bite out of the belly of the crab and started to eat it raw. "Haven't had this shit in a long while."

"Enjoy," Samson said. He turned to Paulo. "You be good for Cobra, okay?"

The boy stared at him. "Don't go."

"You can't come with me, kid."

"Don't go."

Samson patted the boy on the shoulder and got into his car.

He revved the engine, sending dust up into the air. He pulled away, watching the boy in the rearview mirror. Cobra was still eating the crab.

VI.

Paulo watched Samson drive away and then heard Cobra cough. There was a gurgling sound and a crunch.

Cobra's abdomen exploded, and out of it came a crab claw covered in stomach acid and bile. Another claw tore through his rectum. A third thing, not quite a crab claw but definitely made of crab parts, made its way up Cobra's throat and out his mouth, plucking his teeth out. His body was carried away by his new, gory appendages, moving into the desert.

Paulo screamed, jumping and waving his hands so Samson would see. In the distance the car skid, spun a full one hundred and eighty degrees, and sped back in his direction.

The boy ran forward, away from the crab-thing.

Samson's car reached him in seconds, sliding around with the passenger side door already open. "Get in, kid!"

Paulo ran to the car and jumped inside.

"What the hell was that?" Samson said.

The boy shook his head. "I don't know. He was eating the crab and then they just came out of him."

Samson couldn't believe it. One minute he's talking to his friend and the next the man's dead.

"You didn't eat any of the crab, did you?"

"No."

"Good," Samson said, putting the pedal to the floor. "I guess you're coming with me."

CHAPTER FIFTEEN

I.

Three Years Ago

Drac was anointed with fish and motor oil by Simon Revair, pastor and head mechanic of the Church of the Starry Engines.

They had taken Drac, the last son of the Dunwich clan and "souped" him up like they would any machine, any car. It was a dangerous experiment; they had tried it on dozens of young men with occult inclinations but always with disastrous results. All of the test subjects were either deceased or roaming the wasteland as biomechanical deformities from the pits of an automotive hell.

Drac endured the surgery, the incantations, and the blasphemous repairs. He forced himself into a half-sleep state as his veins were pumped with sigil-laden gasoline and mixed with the accursed blood of some shunned ancestor. Dreams came quietly, easily, in the form of winged slabs of neon meat. Their tendrils wrapped around his dream-body and forced him to acknowledge their supreme role in an ancient but advanced patriarchy. He acquiesced to the mysterious mechanolater's repairs.

When it was all done, Drac was dropped back into the cellar of his father's house. He didn't remember much, only the sight and sound of leather-like wings. The cellar was just as his father had left it: full of obscure militaria and esoteric texts wrapped in crumbling desert cloth. A wooden donkey sat in one corner, dusty and staring at Drac with those eyes that implored him to burn the house to the ground and let it all fall into ash.

That night Drac dreamt he was a child. He was at the seashore with his father, walking along the beach. To the right of him was the ocean and to the left there were an array of games, simple machines and archaic automatons, where one could win prizes. There was also a mirrored labyrinth, a spook house and a place that was something in between the two. It was called a scratch house and Drac was instinctively horrified.

His father was in full military attire with his arm around Drac, protecting him from harm. Then without actually falling, Drac hurt his knee on the ground below him. It was an instantaneous wound, bubbling and bloody.

"Daddy, I got a boo-boo."

"Oh, I'm sorry, son," his father said, stooping down to eye-level. He gently lifted Drac's leg and kissed the wound. "All better."

"Thanks, Daddy."

Drac woke up with the eyes of the wooden donkey staring at him, begging to be set on fire.

II.

Drac had met Lord Bing Bong, a weirdo historian of

occult tomes, only once, and that one meeting had left him intrigued.

The man was leader of the Zoners, the group of people insane enough to live in the Zone of Dead Roads, an area ravaged by radioactive winds, marauding killers, fecal floods, and the long-headed freaks known as Yuggs.

As far as anyone could tell, the Yuggs were just another result of radiation but some said they had existed *before* the war and that they only made themselves known after the collapse of normal society. The Yuggs were short and yellow with long skulls that stretched their skin tight over exaggerated foreheads. Their facial features were mostly human but their arms were abnormally long, their legs abnormally short. They traveled mostly in groups, surviving by ritualistically stealing things while chanting in an unintelligible language.

Lord Bing Bong didn't approve of the Yuggs or their noisy thefts. He instructed all of the Zoners to slaughter the freaks on sight. Over the course of just one year, hundreds of Yuggs were captured, tortured, dismembered, and killed. Their body parts were used to cook up a strong hallucinogenic. Lord Bing Bong told Drac he had gotten the recipe for the drug from a large tablet of black plastic he had found emblazoned with bizarre hieroglyphs. After nearly a year of translation, a recipe was unearthed.

Drac didn't have anything against Lord Bing Bong. He was a crazy motherfucker, there was no denying that, but he had shown Drac respect. Though that was probably due to the rare tome Drac had sold him. It had been Drac's father's book, something he had no use for: the 1856 edition of Ian Griffith's *Examination of the Great Space and the Deconstructing of Some Inner Societies*. It was heavy reading, even for Drac.

With their prior meeting in mind, Drac decided he could use his history with Bing Bong to get close to him.

"Guess I'm off to see the Lord," he said, stepping on the gas and keeping his eyes on the tall, disfigured buildings on the horizon. Those buildings marked the boundaries of the Zone of Dead Roads. It was an urban, labyrinthine hell. The Zoners repaved the streets after the war, keeping them smooth and even to ensure that unsuspecting drivers wouldn't hesitate to pass through. The Zoners were always on the lookout for drifters to shoot, stab, rape, impale, or set on fire.

When the Zoners were paving the roads, in their minds they were opening a gateway to important visitors from another world, a world only opened to them after the ingestion of the Yugg hallucinogen.

As he entered the Zone, Drac saw an intimidating group of sentries standing in front of every building on the block. They were naked except for spiked elbow pads and ball gags. Each held a huge gun. Drac saw their eyes turn yellow as they stared at him.

He slowed down and waved his hand out the window, moving his fingers the way Lord Bing Bong had instructed him. It was a bizarre gesture, but one that revealed Drac to be a person of occult knowledge and therefore safe until Bing Bong said differently. Drac was, after all, the son of Willum Dunwich, sergeant in the United States Marine Corps and expert in all things metaphysically obscure and magickal.

The sentries nodded slowly, their eyes turning to black.

Drac drove past them, noticing that things had changed since the last time he had been here. Though the Zone had always looked like an urban cesspool, it had gotten worse. The buildings were still run down but now they were covered in black sludge and railroad spikes. Rusted chains and animal skins hung from the lampposts. There were groups of Zoners on the corner of every block, gesturing conspiratorially as Drac drove past.

The Zoners were made up of people from all age and racial groups. The one common characteristic they shared was an unwavering dedication to removing themselves from the past. They refused to acknowledge the nuclear war but instead used the Yugg hallucinogen to expand their inner worlds.

Drugs weren't the only things the Zoners were obsessed with. When Drac had first ventured into the Zone of Dead Roads, he had noticed that every building had a television on at all times and there was only one movie playing. Each and every day, every Zoner would sit through multiple viewings of *Under Siege 2: Dark Territory.*

He didn't understand Lord Bing Bong and his Zoners, but luckily it didn't really matter. He had been able to trade with them and that was all. But now he had to decide how he was going to kill the man.

Drac was formulating a plan when Mama Hell rammed into his car.

III.

"Fuck you!" screamed Mama Hell as she slammed into that glass-skulled freak, sending him onto the sidewalk where a group of Zoners was watching a television that had been placed on a pile of dead Yuggs.

Mama had never been one to watch television and she wondered why these people would bother to use the limited electricity still being produced by the dwindling number of Silver-owned hydroelectric plants. Didn't they have anything better to do with that power? No, they were only interested in rotting their brains with secular nonsense.

She was delighted to see Drac's car run into the Zoners, spraying the air with blood and body parts. The car hit the television, showering him in sparks and yellow flesh.

Drac's car avoided the building, though, and that pissed Mama off. She grabbed her gun, stuck her hand out the window, and fired several shots. The back of Drac's car was riddled with bullet holes but had sustained no substantial damage.

Mama stayed even with Drac's car as it drove off the sidewalk and back onto the road. Her minivan crashed into the convertible again but this time he was ready for it. A tentacle shot up from underneath the car and punctured the side of the van. Mama tried to steer away but found herself stuck.

"You fucking asshole!" she screamed, interpreting the penetration as some form of automotive rape. That glass-skulled freak was a typical man, using his car to compensate for his lack of manhood.

Underneath her ass, she could feel the tentacle molesting the bottom of her van, tearing pieces off her car while sucking up gasoline. One of her tires was punctured and then another. Mama tried steering away from Drac but it didn't work. The car was out of her control.

Another of Drac's tentacles entered Mama's car but this time straight through the back window. It rooted around, tearing up the seats and upholstery. Mama screamed, cursing that ugly freak to hell, wanting to get her hands on him so she could cut him up with her turtle shell, break open the top of his skull, and piss into it like a champagne glass.

She looked over and saw Drac smiling while waving his fingers at her, taunting her, wanting her to make a move. Mama Hell screamed in fury, cleared her throat, and then hocked a gob of phlegm out the window towards Drac's car. It splattered to the asphalt only to be scraped up and eaten by one of the Zoners who seemed completely oblivious of the death race occurring inches from his nose.

The two racers had driven ten blocks into the Zone of Dead Roads and they were approaching a building that had once been a high school. The Zoners had converted the building into a processing plant for the Yugg hallucinogen. This was also the home of Lord Bing Bong.

Drac's car and Mama's minivan sped across the front lawn of the high school. just as they were approaching the building, Drac retracted his tentacles and made a quick one hundred and eighty degree turn, missing the brick by inches. Mama, on the other hand, crashed directly into the front of the school.

IV.

Samson decided he wouldn't kill Lord Bing Bong.

He had wasted enough time visiting Cobra and it wasn't worth risking his life and Paulo's for some unknown prize. Samson had heard stories about Bing Bong and it wasn't as if the man hadn't done things to deserve a death warrant. Still, who knew what traps Silver had laid, hoping the drivers would take the bait?

What he had to be careful about, though, was making it through the Zone of Dead Roads. If Lord Bing Bong knew Silver had put a price on his head, he might be ready to send out his own bizarre assassins to eliminate the racers.

When they were a mile away from the Zone, Paulo turned to Samson and said, "Why do they call it the Zone of Dead Roads?"

"I think it has something to do with how dangerous it is. People tend to drive through there and they don't come out unless Lord Bing Bong lets them," Samson said, not sure if he sounded convincing enough. It wasn't a total lie. The Zone was truly one of the most dangerous places. But that wasn't the reason for its name.

"Really?" The kid was a shrewd one. His eyes told Samson he knew the whole truth hadn't been told.

"Well…"

Their car approached a burnt down train car with the words *LEROUX RAILWAY COMPANY* painted on the side. Dozens of plastic masks hung from the train car, worn out faces of werewolves, spacemen, vampires, robots, pre-war presidents, and fish-faced monsters.

Samson took the opportunity to change the subject. "Wow, pretty cool masks, huh?"

"Yeah, I guess."

That's when Samson saw the sentries standing around the boundary of the Zone. They were holding their weapons up, itching to blow an outsider's car to bits. But from what Samson had heard, they weren't indiscriminate slaughterers. There was a specific method to Lord Bing Bong's bloodthirsty madness. It was all a hallucinatory game to him and to his Zoners.

"Hang on, kid," Samson said, making a hard right into an alleyway, immediately realizing that it could be a trap. He grabbed a shotgun from the backseat and activated the blow gun on top of the car.

They sped down a street and found themselves sandwiched between storefronts decorated with entrails and others covered with jagged metal spikes. Chain-link fences covered the sidewalk, twisted into spirals. Mutilated children's toys hung from quivering wires.

"Are you going to kill that man?" Paulo said.

"Lord Bing Bong? No, we're not going to kill him."

"Why not?"

Samson took his eyes off the road and looked at the boy. "What do you mean, 'why not'? You want me to kill him?"

Paulo shook his head. "I don't know."

"If someone tries to hurt us, I'll do whatever it takes to keep us safe but that doesn't mean I'm going to hunt someone down just because Silver wants me to."

Paulo started to say something but was interrupted by Samson, "Shhhh."

Someone was following them.

Three women on motorcycles were coming up fast. They were topless, the pale skin on their heavy breasts vibrating with the rumbling of their engines. Black boots covered their legs up to the knees and were met with dirty, denim shorts. Each of the three women had the same hair style: a multicolored bird's nest that spread out in all directions like a sombrero. One of them had a vacuum strapped to her back, the hose extending out like a third arm in front of her.

This was bad news. Samson knew there were a multitude of motorcycle gangs roaming the country but from the look of their hair, these three women had come all the way from Canada. Were they taking orders from Silver or were they following Lord Bing Bong?

That wasn't the only thing to worry about. Samson could

see now that there were people occupying the broken down tenement buildings and collapsed stores he was driving past. Mostly he saw the yellow eyes, unblinking and bright. He had no doubt they had weapons pointed towards the street.

As the roar of the motorcycles grew louder, the topless women hoisted crossbows up onto the handlebars of the bikes.

"Stay down, kid," Samson said. Shots were fired out of one of the buildings. A rusted mailbox exploded ten feet in front of their car but Samson managed to avoid the debris. The motorcycle women surrounded the car and Samson realized he had taken the wrong road. Up ahead there was a gigantic stone wall covered in neon lights.

They were driving into a trap.

CHAPTER SIXTEEN

Yowzah! This is crazy!

Sorry, race fans but we had to say adios to that sweetheart Gabby Peppermint. I'd like to say she went out peacefully but... as you saw, she went out in a blaze of entrails! But, hey, no one said it was going to be easy.

And our other lady racer, Mama Hell, just crashed into a building in the Zone of Dead Roads. Little does she know that building is also the headquarters of Lord Bing Bong himself and I imagine he won't be too pleased.

I.

Six Months Ago

Mama walked into the abandoned mega-church and had a seat in front of the stage. She stared at the banner that hung from the ceiling: *God Wants You to Be Rich.*

"Dear Lord," she said. "Please allow me to prosper and be rich just like all of your flock...."

The door behind her opened and in walked an older man who resembled many of the preachers Mama used to watch on television. He wore a white suit and had hair that looked far too styled to be on a man of his age.

"Excuse me," he said. "Are you the one they call Mama Hell?"

Mama glared at him, aggravated that he had interrupted her private time with her savior. "Who are you?"

"I'm sorry but….are you Mama Hell?"

"Yes I am," she said. "Now what do you want?"

"My name is Enzo and I represent Mr. Silver. You are familiar with him, right?"

Mama nodded.

"Well, he's organizing a major race and he needs all the… god-fearing people he can get," Enzo said. He continued. Mama listened to him while trying to decide whether God would have wanted her to be doing so.

After Enzo was finished, Mama said, "I'll have to pray about it."

"And how long will that take?"

"As long as it has to!" Mama slammed her fist down on the chair next to her. She stared into the man's eyes, forcing him to turn around and walk to the door. Before he opened it, he spoke.

"I'll await your answer."

As she sat alone in what she was sure was the presence of the Lord, Mama Hell contemplated entering the race. There was something strange about it, no doubt, but maybe it was her chance to prosper just as God had wanted her to.

She walked outside to see if she could catch up with the man named Enzo and was shocked to see him defecating in the parking lot. "Pagan," she said, knowing a Christian wouldn't dare do a thing like that.

When Enzo saw her, he didn't stop shitting. He just said, "Make a decision?"

Mama Hell nodded. "I'm in."

Enzo wiped his ass with his handkerchief. "Excellent! Mr. Silver will be pleased."

She watched as he got into his white car and drove away, leaving her to catch a whiff of his shit along with the dusty, wasteland wind.

II.

That bastard.

Mama Hell would have given anything to get her hands on Drac. She would have given up any chance of winning the race if she could just get one good shot at him. But she knew that was unlikely. Her minivan was lodged inside the front of the school, completely totaled. She wasn't going to be able to drive out of there.

It was over.

But what the hell was she going to do? She knew the stories about Lord Bing Bong and the Zoners. She knew they were murderous drug fiends, a gang of homicidal black magicians who sacrificed the Yuggs for their infernal purposes. Mama Hell hated those pagan assholes. Even after a world war, they had betrayed God, whereas she had never lost her faith. God was testing humanity and those Zoners had failed miserably.

The driver's side door was heavily damaged but after a few kicks, Mama Hell got it open and stepped into the foyer of the school. It brought back memories not of her own school days but of the time she had spent protesting the local school system for teaching the theory of evolution.

She grabbed her gun and got out of the car. She was surprised to see the foyer was empty. She had assumed there would be Zoners all over the place, ready to pounce on outsiders. Regardless, she needed to find a safe way out of there. The whole place was giving her satanic vibes.

Hanging from the ceiling were flickering fluorescent lights and on the walls were detailed portraits drawn in brown, yellow, and red ink. Mama Hell glanced at the names under the pictures but didn't recognize any of them: *Sir Josef Polver, Xnoybis IV, Simon Revair.*

Several vending machines had been tipped over and gutted. Flowers were growing inside them. A glass case that used to house athletic trophies was filled with grotesque statues of obese women. They were made of wax, leaves, granite, and bone. Mama Hell resisted the urge to smash those examples of pornographic idolatry.

She walked a few feet down a long hallway filled with lockers, debris, and shoes. The door at the other end of the hall opened slowly with a creak. Out walked a tall, bearded man with a scythe.

She had two options: to run back outside or face the bearded man. Zoners were probably already crowding around outside to examine the crash.

She closed her eyes and said, "Dear God, if you cannot deliver me out of the presence of the ungodly, please grant me the power to die a righteous death. Amen."

Then she raised her gun and fired down the hallway.

III.

Drac knew where Lord Bing Bong lived, that he spent much of his day in the former high school watching *Under Siege 2* and experimenting with ancient texts. Bing Bong would do this while defecating into a copper bowl. He was an accomplished spatilomancer. He told Drac he never made any sort of decision before consulting his "bowl of brown dreams," and writing down the results in his journal.

Drac was thirsty. The gasoline at the station hadn't satisfied him or his car. He needed more. His body craved it. His soul craved it.

Mama Hell's car hadn't satisfied him. He knew Lord Bing Bong kept a gas reserve in his building and luckily he was close. Mama Hell had crashed into it and all he had to do was find a way inside and drain the reserves. Then he'd kill Bing Bong.

He figured the easiest thing to do was get in the same way Mama Hell had. He'd crash right into one of the entrances and drive through the hallways like a runaway train. He'd been in there before and was familiar with the layout. Plus, he had the element of surprise.

An explosion in front of his car sent Drac swerving to the left. He nearly crashed into the brick wall of the school as something else exploded right behind him. From the corner of his eye he saw figures on the roof of the school. Zoners.

He stepped on the gas and sped toward the side entrance, his tentacles reaching out to puncture the building before the car did. In an explosion of brick and glass, Drac drove into the school. A few Zoners had been standing in front of the entrance but were quickly crushed by the car.

"Serves you right!" Drac said, watching as the arm of

one Zoner flew up into the air, splashing into a broken water fountain.

It took Drac all of ten seconds to stumble upon a tall, bearded man holding a scythe. The man didn't acknowledge the tentacled car but turned and shuffled slowly down the hall. What the hell was going on?

A bullet exploded the plaster next to Drac's left shoulder. He whipped around to see Mama Hell, shooting her gun with her mouth opened wide, her clothes torn and burnt. She was closing in on the man with the scythe and Drac was slightly tempted to take the man down so he could finish off Mama himself.

Instead, he just watched.

IV.

"You godless piece of shit!" Mama Hell screamed. She was shooting so regularly, the act was as natural as breathing. But the Zoner with the scythe still came towards her. She didn't hear the roar of Drac's engine until she saw the car swinging around the corner down the hall.

She wasn't too happy about that. Now she had two assholes to deal with.

Then she was out of bullets. The scythe-Zoner grunted in satisfaction. A hellish burp escaped from his mouth. He licked his lips and spoke, "Lord doesn't wish to speak to you, bitch."

Mama Hell's eyes turned into hateful slits. Her gun was now useless, but she did have other weapons in the car. She just needed to run back and get one…

She ran, cursing the bearded bastard. But he followed after, waving his weapon in front of him, slashing at Mama Hell. She had reached her car and was grabbing for the door when she felt a sharp pain in her back.

The scythe had caught her, ripping skin off. But luckily for Mama Hell, it wasn't her skin.

The tattooed vest of flesh had saved her life. The Zoner thought he had her, thought she was wounded when he saw that pancake of skin fall off. It gave Mama Hell just enough time to jump into the driver's side of the car and grab her razor-sharp turtle shell which she quickly whirled at the Zoner.

It hit him in the neck.

He dropped the scythe, his hands reached up, trying to plug the hole that was gushing copious amounts of blood onto his chest and feet. For a second, it looked as if he was draped in a red robe.

Mama Hell laughed loudly. She walked over to the bleeding man, kicked him in the crotch and took his scythe.

The man died holding his neck and groin.

Mama Hell picked up her skin vest and wrapped it around herself. She laughed as she walked away with the dead man's weapon. That's when she heard the roar of Drac Dunwich's car. He was coming right towards her.

V.

Drac didn't expect Mama Hell to survive the fight with the Zoner. The Zoners were impervious to pain, even gunshots, when they were high on their Yugg drug. He revved his engine, preparing to speed down the hall and into the bearded Zoner but then he saw Mama Hell turn the corner holding the scythe.

Shit, the bitch survived.

Oh well. He had no qualms about running her down. She was a thorn in his side and a despicable example of a human being. He was going to take great pleasure in making her road kill.

He put the car in gear and sped down the hallway. There was no way that woman was going to be able to move out of the way fast enough. He stared her down as he went straight for her.

Mama Hell must have just given up. She didn't even make an attempt to move out of the way as Drac's car pummeled her into the cinderblock. Drac stepped on the brake fast enough not to total his car. Mama Hell, on the other hand, was totaled. She was cut cleanly in half, her bottom half slid to the ground beneath the fender.

Her top half was on the hood of Drac's car. She was still conscious, gripping the scythe with all her might. Her mouth was foaming.

"Godless freak!" she said. The red tattoos on her skin-vest were moving now, swirling into shapes: a devil, a dwarf, a deck of cards, a sun, a question mark, a bungalow, an obelisk, a spiral, a winged creature.

The scythe slammed down into the windshield, causing a slight fracture. Drac grabbed his gun, stuck his hand out the window, and fired at Mama's head. It exploded like a godly sunburst.

"Freak?" Drac said. "I'm not a freak."

CHAPTER SEVENTEEN

I.

Samson pressed the button between the seats and from out of the back of his car came a deluge of white foam.

The vacuum-woman riding behind the car was knocked off her motorcycle by the force of the foam. She hit the ground like a sack of rocks. The vacuum exploded, opening a gaping hole in her back. Organs, ribs, vacuum parts, and white foam covered the street.

The other two women looked back in surprise, giving Samson a chance to step on the brakes and watch as they raced past him. He quickly aimed the blowgun and shot the women off their bikes, their breasts flapping like overused pin cushions.

With a quick turn of the steering wheel, Samson avoided the lighted brick wall and brought the car down an alley to the left only to be confronted with another group of Zoners.

They had hoisted a Yugg above their heads, long flat knives waved around in the air. They were about to skin it alive.

"Close your eyes, kid," Samson said. Paulo slapped his hands over his face.

The car plowed into the Zoners. Several heavy thumps rocked the car. One of them hung onto the hood, staring into the windshield at Samson. He was a particularly ugly Zoner with a patchy beard and bug eyes. One of his hands was clutching the car, while the other held a handful of Yugg flesh. The Zoner slapped the flesh onto the windshield.

"Is this your lunch?" he said to Samson. The Zoner put the meat to his face and snorted flakes of flesh up into his nose. "Once you get used to it…it just clears the sinuses!"

Samson slammed on the brake and the Zoner went flying forward, his skull hitting the ground and opening like a rotten pumpkin.

Paulo uncovered his eyes and stared out at the corpse. He watched as the asphalt bubbled like a bowl of black pudding and swallowed up the dead Zoner. The boiling road let out a monstrous burp.

Samson put the car in reverse. "Now you know why it's called the Zone of Dead Roads."

II.

Drac drove down the halls of the school, his tentacles ripping the lockers off the walls. The element of surprise was out of the question and now he just wanted the gasoline. Killing Lord Bing Bong was second on the list of priorities. If the man was willing to let Drac drain the reserves, then his life might be spared. After all, they did know each other. Bing Bong just might let Drac have the gas for old time's sake. If not, well…

The man would just have to die.

"Pure road hell brutality," Drac said over and over to himself, gripping the steering wheel and letting his anger take control. It was an anger that forced him to delve into his psyche, his gasoline-laden memories, and pick through painful scenes. An image of his body being melted into another. His limbs being doused in sludge. An oil-soaked trapezohedron.

A rock hit his windshield, knocking him back into reality.

He slammed on the brakes and set the car in reverse, passing a small man standing in the doorway of a classroom. The man was wearing a football helmet and a navy uniform that was splattered with a neon liquid. His face was covered in a mask of concentric wrinkles, a whirlpool of age engraved in between intense eyes and a fat-lipped mouth.

Drac stopped in front of the man and stuck his head out of the window. He laughed, a high-pitched sound that reverberated down the hallway. The sight of little Lord Bing Bong was quite humorous.

"You're lucky my windshield isn't broken," he said.

"Dunwich, you better have a good reason for being on my train," Lord Bing Bong said, his bulbous lips dripping bright green drool.

"Train?" Drac realized the man had gotten more insane since the last time they had met. "No train. But listen. I need gasoline. I assumed since we had done business before you might be inclined to…"

"ASSUMPTION IS THE MOTHER OF ALL FUCK UPS!" Lord Bing Bong screamed, getting close to the car and sticking his head inside.

The two men stared at each other, Drac smiling slyly while Bing Bong frowned sloppily.

"So are you going to give me the gasoline or what?" Drac tapped on his temple with his finger. "I don't like getting this close to empty."

"You need to get off my train before I kill you," Lord Bing Bong said.

Drac leaned back in the driver's seat. "You know who I am. You know who my father was. You and I, we've done business."

"I don't care *who* your father was." Lord Bing Bong punched his football helmet with both hands. "I don't fucking *care!*"

"Listen, Lord, I know you have a lot to handle, taking care of all the Zoners and dealing with the Yuggs and all that but I'm asking as a favor."

"A favor? In this world of shit you ask for a favor? Let me tell you, since you are so concerned with who your father was, let me tell you who *my* father was."

"I'm not concerned with that."

"If you want me to consider a favor, then you will be concerned. Understand?"

Drac shook his head.

"My father, he was a man of respect, you know that, moved us from Palermo when I was just a boy. You know what my first lesson was when coming to this shit country?"

"What?"

"My father took me to a train yard and locked me in one of the cars, told me I had to think about how grateful I should be, to be in this new country with new opportunities. I thought about it alright, I thought about how I wish I was pouring cement in Palermo, putting my father in that same cement. Let him suffocate slowly, let his lungs harden up. That's what I thought about in there, locked in the train car for two days with nothing to keep me company except for a fucking comic book I had in my back pocket. Spent two days thinking about killing my father and reading about a fucking cartoon donkey."

Drac could see Lord Bing Bong unraveling in front of his eyes. The wrinkles on his face transformed into obscure sigils and his lips turned deep red.

The two men stared at each other.

Finally Drac said, "I'm not sure I understand your point."

"When my father finally came to get me out, you know what he said? He said that I should be grateful. That he did me a favor. A fucking *favor*. So please pardon me if I'm not partial to that word."

"I apologize if I hit a nerve but what if I said I had some books in my trunk, books I'd let you take a look at for a possible trade." Drac smiled widely, showing yellow teeth. "*Rare* books."

Lord Bing Bong's frown lessened and he moved his head out of the car. He put his hands on his hips. "I don't know what I'd say. It would depend on what you had. Let me see and maybe I'll let you take some gasoline off my train."

Drac reached down, pulled a lever, and popped the trunk. He nodded with his head for Bing Bong to go check it out. "I think you'll find something of interest back there. I traded with a Yugg for some pretty obscure texts."

Bing Bong's face turned red. "I'll bet you your goddamn car they're my books that were stolen by those ugly abominations. Two weeks ago my copy of the *Abgrund Abschaum* went missing. Books don't just get up and walk away. Then this week someone took the *Yonimani Yantra Fragments*.....right from underneath my nose! I bet you it was those fucking Yuggs!"

"I assure you, I do not have any stolen books in my possession," Drac said. He motioned to his trunk. "But feel free to check for yourself."

Lord Bing Bong grunted and made his way to the back of the car. He put his hand on the trunk and lifted it.

A tentacle shot out, impaling him.

It waved him into the air while he screamed. "You stupid fucking bastard! You think you're getting out of my train alive now? You think the Zoners are going to let you leave? You son of a bitch!"

Drac watched in his rearview mirror as the tentacle flapped the man around, banging him against the walls so hard the football helmet cracked into his skull. With brains pouring out of his head, Lord Bing Bong spoke.

"That is not dead which can eternal lie," the dying man said. "And with strange engines even death may drive."

III.

"Where are we going?" Paulo said. He was visibly shaken from witnessing the asphalt devour the Zoner.

"To the finishing line," Samson said. "Atlantic City."

"We're not going to kill Bing Bong?"

"Nope."

Samson was driving fast through the streets of the Zone, marveling at how ominous the buildings looked now that he had had a glimpse of the horrors beneath them. Were the rumors true? There were many stories about the Zoners and their mixing Yugg remains in with the tar when they repaved the streets. It was strange to Samson how they could take something as common as road-paving and turn it into something so morbid and perverse.

There were still people watching him from inside the

buildings. Televisions were still playing, all the same movie. On the streets there were Zoners smoking large cigars made of Yugg scalps. The smoke from them rose slower than normal smoke and twisted into shiny spirals.

Some of the Zoners were wearing backpacks and looked like overgrown college kids whereas others were dressed in filthy, military attire. They were all armed, all preoccupied with something, almost meditative in their demeanor.

As he drove down the streets, Samson realized something. No one was trying to attack. He had expected there to be at the least some more topless motorcycle women or some zealous Zoners on foot who would want to strike but there was nothing but distracted inhabitants, just like any city before the war.

"What's wrong?" Paulo said, seeing the worry on Samson's face.

"I don't know, kid. I guess I was expecting more, you know, danger, people trying to kill us. Now everything seems so…"

"Quiet?"

"Yeah, quiet. But I don't think that's a good thing."

IV.

After draining the gasoline reserves, Drac drove away, leaving Lord Bing Bong's shredded body in the hallway of the "train" and the football helmet still hanging off one of the tentacles.

Drac was on the streets in minutes. But the Zoners weren't attacking. They seemed unaware of what had happened at the school. But it wasn't just that. They seemed completely oblivious to everything. Drac drove up onto a sidewalk, letting the tentacles pick up a few spacey Zoners, whip them around and toss them back down. It was as if Bing Bong's death had destroyed any motivation they might have had. That was fine by Drac. He didn't need any more trouble.

One thing that worried him was that the buildings seemed taller than before. Each one reached up like a finger aching to puncture the clouds.

Drac shook his head. Why was he always so paranoid? It had something to do with his father. Something about… The memories were there but they weren't clear. There was never enough to give him any substantial amount of introspection.

But he had to focus. He had to get safely out of the Zone of Dead Roads and reach Atlantic City first. The race was the one thing he was sure about. He had to win. He wasn't concerned about the supplies, or even the gasoline (his tentacles found plenty of that on the road). It was the city that had risen off the coast.

R'lyeh.

He had to get there. He was drawn there. Something about it was so familiar. Had his father talked about it? Was it in one of his books? There was a sense of ecstatic danger like a child standing in front of a roller coaster for the first time.

But there was the problem of Mr. Silver. There was something wrong with that man. It wasn't the bloodthirsty exploitation of his fellow survivors. There was more to it than that. Silver had a disturbing confidence, almost a power, that Drac had only seen in one other person: his father.

CHAPTER EIGHTEEN

I.

Five Years Ago

Long before Samson was approached by Enzo, he had already earned himself a reputation as one of the fastest drivers in New Jersey and the surrounding wasteland towns. It started as an accident.

After his wife took his car, Samson walked from town to town, doing small jobs for colonies of people hoping to begin anew. He mostly helped dig for well water, harvesting crops that were mutated beyond the level of safe consumption. But he didn't mind. He did whatever it took to get his mind off his son.

At some point Samson decided to venture into the Pennsylvanian Wastelands. There were large towns there, mostly nuclear slums, radioactive ghettoes; places where the black market was teeming with anything anyone might need to replicate pre-war normality. Samson had heard about a town called Dogunville that had been constructed out of cement blocks by a man named LeRoux. LeRoux had spray painted each block with elaborate and violent scenes. He told people the scenes were from movies and comics featuring demonic heroes and tortured villains, perverse power plays involving fetishistic psychodramas. Childhood trauma was imprinted upon cement like a series of vivid flashbacks. After LeRoux built up the walls of the town, he retreated into a yellow bunker full of canned food and DVDs.

Samson heard the stories and had been tempted to go there, to indulge in the bizarre theater of Dogunville, so he mustered up the energy and hitched a ride in an old man's truck. They road for five hours, luckily dodging a gang of marauders who were too interested in getting drunk off their newly acquired bottle of antifreeze to bother with Samson and the old man.

When he was dropped off at Dogunville, Samson gave the old man a small can of vegetables as payment. The man accepted the trade and gave him one warning. He said, "Whatever you do, watch out for the guy with the cars." Samson nodded and walked into the heart of the town.

The rumors had been true. The city, every building and every house, was made out of cement blocks, each with a different scene painted on them in bright paint. Samson thought it was refreshing after the dark, dull towns that were being rebuilt in New Jersey out of wood and discarded sheet metal. Dogunville seemed alive, attuned to the human imagination. Still, it was a post-apocalyptic town like any other so he knew he had to be careful.

The people looked friendly enough. They were dirty and exhausted, probably from building up another cement structure. Their tired faces reminded Samson of the pictures of his great-grandparents taken before they immigrated to America from Sicily. Life had been difficult, it had beaten them daily, but they had found pleasure in the struggle.

Samson walked to the main square of the town where an ancient man was arranging half-rotten fruit on a table. It was at that moment, while looking at a few neon-green pears, that he realized there was no good reason why he had come to Dogunville. Hitching a ride from a stranger, coming this far simply because he had heard about some bizarre art painted on cement, that just wasn't like him. But as he looked at the pictures, he felt a switch being flipped. The pictures he saw seemed more like memories than anything else.

They weren't the memories he wanted. Samson wanted to cherish the memories of his son and the times they played games together, told stories to each other. From a very early age Jack had been a good storyteller. When he was five, he made up a tale about cannibalistic dwarves from outer space that came to earth to help the United States fight in the Vietnam War. Samson had been amused by the story but, as always, his wife had disapproved of such a grotesque use of the boy's creativity.

They might have been gruesome but Samson wanted to remember those stories. They reminded him that his son had not just been his offspring but a separate person with thoughts, dreams, and a vivid imagination. Samson cherished that. It made him want to track down the men who took his son. But where would he have looked? Tomato Joe and his gang could have been on the West Coast Wasteland for all he knew.

Samson pointed to the pear and asked the man how much it was.

"Whatta ya got?" the old man answered.

"Just a few things. Looking for anything in particular?"

The old man grinned. "Oh, I could really use some toys, you know, to entertain the kiddies. They're sick of looking at the cement."

Samson opened his satchel and looked through his supplies. Aside from dried meat, canned food, bottles of water, and some magazines, he did have a few toys.

Jack's toys.

They had been in his bag since the day Jack was taken. His son was always asking him to carry a Matchbox car or a one-armed action figure. Samson had no problem with that. But now there they were, two brightly painted die-cast metal cars at the bottom of the satchel all alone with no child to push them along.

"I don't have any toys," Samson said. "Sorry."

"Oh?" The man leaned his head forward and widened his eyes. "Well, that's too bad for you, eh? This fruit is, how do I put it? Delicious. But maybe you'd like something else, something cheaper? I might have some…tomatoes."

Samson could see something in the man's face, something like secret and sinister knowledge. He was about to inquire further when a hand gripped his shoulder.

"Don't listen to the old man. He's a fucking loon."

Samson turned quickly to look at who had touched him. Standing there was a young man, someone who looked like he didn't quite belong in the town. His hair was short and clean, as if it had been washed and cut recently. Bright blue eyes stared out from a handsome face. The man's clothing was also unusual: a silver jumpsuit with a sun insignia on the right shoulder.

"Hands off, okay?" Samson said, moving himself away from both men. The old vendor muttered a curse but the young man followed him.

"Hey, meant no harm. Just trying to help you avoid trouble. Looked like you were about to hit him," the young man said.

Samson kept walking. "Well, I wasn't going to."

"Okay, okay. I'll be honest with you. I was hoping we could make a trade."

"What?" Samson stopped. He should have known that's what this was about, a goddamn trade. Everything was a trade or a gamble or a con. "A trade for what?"

"What do you want? You said it yourself you don't have any toys. You want some? I got some. Got a Rubik's Cube, some board games, some Boglins. I don't have kids, but well, maybe someday. I might have to build one myself." He laughed. "Maybe you want some food, some meat, some magazines, girls. Shit, I got a lot."

"Well, I don't have much to trade," Samson said.

"What? Maybe you're not interested in all that, fine. But I got cars, man. Real cars, not toys. I saw you didn't drive here. You had to hitch a ride from some trucker. So maybe you need a car."

Samson shook his head and looked around. The cement paintings were overwhelming. It was just scene after scene of elaborate violence and inenarrable sex involving obscure shapes and horrified faces. Train wrecks, flesh pistols, car crashes, marital discord, and joyful assassinations. He thought he saw some paintings of dwarves in a jungle…holding guns in front of a spaceship.

"Hey, what's the matter?" the young man's voice broke Samson's concentration.

"What?"

"You looked messed up, man. You need something? You a Zoner? You need drugs or something? I can get you some."

"No, no drugs," Samson said. He blinked a few times, looked over at the cement paintings, but did not see the dwarves again. "What's this about a car?"

"I got lots of cars, man. Lots of them," he said. "I just need a guy to help me do some work. Nothing major, just putting together some machines. It's going to take me a while if I do it by myself and all these people in town are too preoccupied with all this cement shit. If they're not staring at those pictures, they're reading old Tom Clancy novels. So I need all the help I can get. You in?"

Samson thought about it. The offer wasn't uncommon. Oftentimes people in towns would hire outsiders to help them with tasks no one else would assist with. It was usually back-breaking work rewarded by a rare but near worthless token of payment like a bag of jewelry, a paperback book, or a can of creamed corn.

"Yeah, guess so."

"Great." The young man brought Samson to a large yard enclosed by cement slabs. A dilapidated Victorian house stood up from the yard in the midst of a dozen cars, all freshly waxed and weaponized.

"Wow."

"Yeah, rebuilt them all myself." The young man winked. "Well, maybe with a little help."

"So all I got to do is help you with something."

"Oh yeah, you help me with something and when we're done, all you got to do is look at all the cars," the young man said, waving his hand at the cars. "Then…choose."

It took Samson close to six hours of work helping the man. Though he followed the man's directions carefully, he had no clue what the task actually was. He moved a lot of machine parts, old manuals, plastic tubing, glass domes of all sizes, metal pipes, cans of liquid, and unidentifiable junk. Samson felt like he was in a haze. He could hear the man's directions and could feel his body following the directions but he felt like there was another part of him daydreaming. While hauling the equipment, Samson's peripheral vision was clouded by dull light.

Once they were done, the young man patted Samson on the back and said, "You've been a big help. Thanks."

Without any questions, Samson walked over to a car that was in the middle of the yard. It was so appealing, it made Samson feel ashamed for not having noticed it earlier. It had obviously been custom made but it looked almost biological in its construction. He said, "That one."

The young man laughed. "Well then, I guess our trade is over." He showed Samson around the car and explained the various intricacies of its operation. There was a lot to take in, considering it had been equipped with custom weapons.

Afterwards, Samson took the keys and thanked the man. Then he said, "Hey, I never got your name. I'm Samson."

The young man looked up into the sky, his bright blue eyes turning dark and said, "I'm Simon Revair."

II.

While making their way out of the Zone of Dead Roads, Samson taught Paulo how to use a gun.

The boy learned quickly and that was a good thing. Samson mentally kicked himself for not doing it earlier. The race was only going to get tougher and he might need an extra set of hands even if those hands were young ones wielding a deadly weapon.

"I think you've got it, kid. Now just don't point the thing

at me, okay?" Samson laughed.

"Okay."

"And don't worry, I don't think we're going to be seeing many more of those Zoners. We're almost to Atlantic City. We're going to see a whole different type of creepy people."

"Who?"

"Spectators."

"What's that mean?"

"The audience. The people who are watching us right now." Samson pointed at cameras attached to the obsolete telephone poles along the side of the road. They were also placed on billboards, buildings, and trees.

"People are…watching us?"

"Yeah, kid. All this we've been doing, it's entertainment for them." Samson had briefly told Paulo about the race before but it looked like the boy didn't grasp the full concept of it, that they were involved in a blood sport, a death race. If they reached Atlantic City and were the losers of the race, there was a good possibility the audience would tear them apart because they had failed to succeed. Ironically, if they were the winners, they might be torn apart anyway in the rabid, bloodthirsty fanfare. And Mr. Silver would love every second of it.

"Are we winning?" Paulo said.

"I don't know. Maybe. I just hope we make it there alive." Samson regretted saying it as soon as it came out of his mouth. He saw Paulo wince.

"Me, too," the boy said, turning to the window.

They drove down the highway that connected Atlantic City to the rest of New Jersey. Though the area wasn't inhabited, the highway itself was home to various mutated animals who sought haven in the potholes.

On the horizon, Samson saw Atlantic City, neon-bright even in daytime. The buildings were crooked fingers, a few bending over onto their neighbors. They were mostly former casino hotels, a thing of the pre-war past, and a reminder of carefree vices. On the tops of the buildings, huge yellow flags waving slowly in the wind. To Samson they looked like huge, heavy slices of golden flesh.

As they drove closer, zig-zagging around the potholes and scurrying two-headed rabbits, Samson and Paulo both gasped at the sight of something coming into their field of vision. Though it was mostly blocked by the casinos, the object was emanating a striking, dark green glow that threw everything before it into violent shadow.

Samson's bowels churned. He took his foot off the gas pedal and let the car coast around the potholes.

"What is that?" Paulo said.

"R'lyeh," Samson said. "It's R'lyeh."

III.

Five Years Ago

Samson had a car. He had a purpose. He was going to get his son back.

Despite the lack of any real long distance communication, word traveled fast through post-war America. Stories were told and rumors were spread from trade bus to caravan to wasteland towns.

For two years Samson asked around about a biker named Tomato and received bits and pieces of information. Some bits conflicted with others but what he did find out was that there was a guy named Tomato Joe who led a group of bikers and the last time anyone saw him, he was headed to north Jersey.

When Samson had heard this from three different people, he drove his car through New Jersey, stopping only to gather more information on Tomato Joe. For some time Samson had been preparing himself with a strict fitness regimen consisting of push-ups, sit-ups, and lifting whatever heavy objects he could find: small boulders, engine blocks, tires. Though never much of a fighter before, he practiced punching into sand, glass, and asphalt. He hit himself in the face again and again. The pain didn't matter. He wanted to make himself immune to it.

Eventually Samson met a man named Marsh who operated a small trading post in what used to be the city of New Providence. Marsh was dark and wrinkled, so much so that at first Samson thought the man was wearing a mask.

"You hear of a biker named Tomato Joe?" he had asked Marsh.

The man squinted, the wrinkles on his face turning into a map of ancient despair. His throat gargled. "Tomato Joe, you say?"

"That's what I said."

"You a friend of his?"

"Not exactly."

Marsh nodded. "Good. He's a piece of shit."

"I know."

"Last I heard he went over to Jersey City. Don't know if he's still there but that's what I heard."

"Did you see him?"

"Saw him a while ago. Why?"

"Did he have anyone with him?"

"Just those goddamn bikers of his."

"No, I mean…other people."

Marsh looked up at the sky and then at Samson. "You trying to say he took someone?"

Samson nodded. "Yeah. Do you remember if he had anyone with him like…a kid?"

Marsh said, "Couldn't really tell you either way. Maybe he did, I don't know. It wouldn't be the first time. He always does that sort of thing, takes people, sells 'em. I know he's been in business with Silver for a while."

"Silver."

"Yep," Marsh said. "Now, you gonna buy something or what?"

Samson appeased the man and bought a few cans of provisions. Then he sped off to Jersey City in search of Tomato Joe.

CHAPTER NINETEEN

Wow! This race is surprising even me and I've seen a lot of shit, lemme tell you!

Mama Hell is now in...well, I'd like to think she's in heaven, right? I mean, she was a good, God-fearing woman. But she sure as hell got the brunt of Drac's "pure road hell brutality." Boy did they make a mess in Lord Bing Bong's place.

And speaking of Lord Bing Bong, did everyone see him get gut-fucked by Drac's tentacle? Shit, I haven't seen a death like that since Howie Myers got gutted by Chainsaw Cook. Now that was a mess! So Drac wins the special prize and we'll all find out what that is when he reaches Atlantic City.

But who's going to win this electrifying death race, eh? I don't know. Your guess is as good as mine!

I.

Drac thought he was in first place until he saw the exhaust from Samson's car about a half mile ahead.

"Son of a bitch," he said, half-heartedly. He was glad it was Samson he'd be facing in the last leg of the race. There was something about the man that Drac respected.

He sped up, navigating around the potholes and the freakish animals running across the road, almost daring him to turn them into radioactive road kill. He opened the top of his convertible and locked the gas pedal down. He stood on the driver's seat, crouching down just enough to be able to steer the car with one hand. With the other he held his giant, white gun.

Then the eerie light of R'lyeh rose over the horizon.

He nearly fell out of the car. The ancient city, rising up from behind the casino hotels, struck fear into him. He steadied himself.

He had to keep driving.

With a high-pitched scream, Drac Dunwich cocked his gun and steered around the potholes towards Samson's car.

II.

One Year Ago

Jersey City was a shitty place before the war so there wasn't much of a contrast when Samson drove into town. Dilapidated housing and burnt out urban areas made up much of the landscape. In the center was the Northern Compound, but that was off limits to everyone unless they had specific permission to enter from the gangster warlord himself, Mr. Silver.

Samson wasn't interested in Silver, though. He was looking for Tomato Joe.

Most of the population of Jersey City was heavily into drugs. That wasn't strange for a post-war city. The war had turned the country upside down and those who already had unstable lives found themselves pushed into any available form of escape.

He drove slowly through the streets, looking for any sign of Tomato's biker gang. At the sound of a motorcycle in the distance, he stopped the car and rolled down the window to listen.

Yeah, it was a motorcycle engine. But then: a click and a voice.

"Get outta the fuckin car, asshole," it said, a high-pitched whisper.

Samson turned his head to the left and saw a guy in a reverse mohawk standing there with a small revolver pointed at him. He was really just a kid, couldn't have been more than sixteen, seventeen years old. Samson shook his head slightly. It was a shame.

"Just back up, kid," he said. "I've got no business with you."

The punk nodded quickly, causing the numerous metal rings on his face to jingle. His lips quivered and drool leaked out of a hole in his chin. "Oh yeah? Yeah?"

"Yeah."

The punk cocked the revolver.

"Well, maybe I got business with you, old man."

Samson didn't want to do it but it seemed like the only option. "Just walk the fuck away."

From behind a car, another voice shouted, "What's taking so long, Trash?"

The punk with the revolver turned his head, just a little bit, and said, "Shut the hell up, Ogre!"

Samson saw his chance. While Trash's attention was on his friend, he grabbed his own gun and shot the punk in the chest. He started the car and stepped on the gas. In the rearview mirror he saw the guy named Ogre kneeling by his bleeding comrade and shaking his fist at Samson.

The motorcycle sound had multiplied. Samson rounded a corner, almost running down a junkie waving a red and black flag.

Then he saw them. "Bingo."

The motorcycle gang was coming right for him. Samson recognized a few of them. How could he forget? They all wore the same patches as Tomato Joe's gang. Bullwhips wrapped around their necks.

He put the gas pedal to the floor and sped up towards the gang, swerving to the right, and knocking into them. Two of the bikers flew off their vehicles and onto the sidewalk while two others drove straight into a storefront.

Samson didn't see Tomato Joe but he was sure going to find out where the guy was. He turned his car around and got out of it, holding his gun in one hand and a baseball bat in the other. The nearest biker lay on the ground with a broken leg. One of his ribs jutted out of his white t-shirt.

Samson walked up to him and hit him across the face with the bat. "Bowsman."

The biker screamed. "What the fuck, man!"

"You don't remember me?" Samson said. "I remember you…Bowsman."

The other biker was reaching for something. Samson shot him in the face. He looked back down at Bowsman and lifted the bat.

Bowsman said, "What the fuck you doing, man?"

"Where's my son?"

"Who?"

"My son." Samson hit him in the chest, the wooden bat

making contact with the exposed rib.

The biker screamed. "Shit, man, I don't know what the fuck you're talking about."

"What about Tomato Joe? Where is he?"

"Fuck you, man!"

Another hit to the rib.

"Where is he?"

"Okay, fuck, man. He's at Goehrig's."

"Where's that?"

"Down the road, man. Place that says 'bakery' on it." Bowsman grimaced and rolled over, his rib scraping against the sidewalk, sending chills up Samson's spine.

"Does he still have a boy with him?"

"Man, you're crazy."

Samson put his gun in his waistband and held the baseball bat with two hands. He swung it at Bowsman's shoulder, dislocating it. "Fine, I'm crazy."

From behind him, Samson could hear the other two bikers climbing out of the storefront rubble. He grabbed his gun and swung it in their direction. "Just stay where you are, assholes."

They nodded. Both of their heads were cut and they were bleeding profusely.

Samson got into his car and put it in reverse, backing up a half a block. Then he sped up onto the sidewalk and ran over Bowsman.

He drove up the road and found the building that said Goehrig's Bakery. The windows were boarded up and the front was spray-painted with graffiti: *Free the Noid, Frankie Booth waz hair, SNIPERZ says Sit Still, Jack's Back.*

There was a motorcycle parked in front. Samson parked next to it and got out of the car, his gun in one hand and the baseball bat in the other.

He opened the front door and walked into darkness.

A quiet and exhausted voice said, "Bowsman, that you?"

Samson stood still. "Nope, not Bowsman."

"Mayo?"

"Nope."

"Ingmar?"

"Guess again."

"Who the fuck then?"

Samson walked towards the voice, through a hallway, and into a large kitchen. There he was: Tomato Joe. He was sitting at a table in front of a giant oven. The man was skinny, shirtless, with a needle poised to plunge into his arm.

"You don't look like much," Samson said.

"Fuck are you?"

"I guess you don't remember."

"No. Should I?"

"Bowsman didn't remember either," Samson said, stepping closer so Tomato Joe could get a better look. "So I ran him over with my car."

"Listen, asshole, get the fuck out of here." He looked down at the syringe and emptied the contents into his vein.

The baseball bat slammed down on his forearm, cracking it. Blood and drugs splattered the table.

"Where's my son?" Samson said, lifting the bat and slamming it into Tomato Joe's chest, knocking him backward to the floor.

Samson stood over him, pointing the gun at Tomato's face.

"I don't know what you're talking about. What son?"

"My son. You took him. I was driving with my family on

the road and you pulled us over. You took him away. Where did you take him?"

Tomato Joe looked sincerely confused. "What do you mean? When was this? When did this happen?"

"Two years ago."

"You expect me to remember shit like that?" Tomato Joe started to get to his feet, holding his arm and gritting his teeth. "I think you broke my fucking arm."

The baseball bat hit Tomato Joe in the neck. He screamed.

"How's that?" Samson said. He swung it again, hitting the biker in the balls.

"Fuck!"

"The people you kidnap. The kids. Where do you bring them?"

"Fuck off, asshole."

Another hit with the bat. Samson realized that post-war bikers were a stubborn bunch. Just like Bowsman, it was going to take more pain to make Tomato Joe talk.

"Where do you take them?"

"To hell."

Samson threw himself onto Tomato Joe, kneeing him in the balls and holding the baseball bat against his throat. "I can make this last a long, long time. Now tell me where you bring the kids."

"Different places, man. I don't remember every single one. I don't know what the hell I did with him. You want me to tell you he ended up in some nice family? Well I don't know. Maybe he did. But he could have ended up with some chicken hawk freak or something. Who gives a fuck?" Tomato Joe laughed, blood spilling out of his mouth along with yellow foam. The drugs had taken a toll.

"You're a fucking waste of life, you know that?"

Tomato Joe chuckled. "Yeah, I know."

Samson put the gun to the man's head and cocked it.

"Some of the kids, you know, they end up being bought by Silver."

"Really?"

"Yeah, he buys the kids sometimes. I don't remember which ones but some of them."

"What does he do with them?"

Tomato Joe shook his head weakly. "The hell would I know? The guy's a fucking maniac. But if he does have your son, you can sure as hell kiss him goodbye. You ain't seeing him again. That's for sure."

"Shut up," Samson said. He pulled the trigger.

III.

Even over the roar of his car's engine, Samson could hear Drac's scream. The guy was coming up fast, standing on his front seat like a gladiator on a chariot.

"Get down, kid," he said to Paulo.

Samson grabbed the handle of the blowgun and looked into the rearview mirror, trying to aim the best he could. When he had the other driver in his sights, he pressed the trigger. Dozens of sharp needles shot out of the blowgun and struck Drac.

Unfortunately, most of them hit his head and were deflected by the glass skull. Drac fired several shots, shattering the back window of Samson's car.

"Watch out!" Paulo screamed. He had been peeking out

the window and was pointing towards a black rabbit the size of a cow that was sitting in the middle of the road. Samson swerved to miss it but hit the edge of a pothole, knocking his car to the side of the road.

Drac avoided the pothole but not the rabbit. His car crashed through the thing, tentacles ripping it apart, spreading entrails across the road in a neon explosion of bloody confetti. He sat down in his seat and sped past Samson, who was trying to get his car onto the road.

Both cars were coming up to the entrance of Mr. Silver's Atlantic City compound but Drac was ten feet ahead. Samson got back onto the road, glass still falling like snowflakes from the back of his car. He was gaining on Drac but he hit another pothole, causing him to lose a few precious feet.

Up ahead was a huge gate with a ribbon tied to each end. The finish line.

IV.

Six Months Ago

Samson was sitting on the hood of his car, flipping through a handful of Garbage Pail Kids cards he had found in, of all places, a trashcan. He thought they might be worth trading.

His car was parked at an abandoned rest stop off the Garden State Parkway right outside of Jersey City where many races were held. He had to do something, anything to keep him from thinking about his son. The last few years had been spent tracking down clues about Jack's whereabouts, all that had led nowhere. Racing was such an easy distraction.

On that particular day, there was no one around. Samson

was about to leave when he heard an engine in the distance. Down the road he saw a white jalopy making its way to him, slow and rickety. He grabbed his gun as it parked next to his car. A man in a white suit got out of the car.

"Hello there," the man said. "You Samson?"

"Who wants to know?"

"My name is Enzo. I represent Mr. Silver. You do know who Mr. Silver is, correct?"

"Yeah, I heard of him."

"You've raced for him…whether you know it or not. He's noticed you. Your win against Savage Freddie was nothing short of amazing. Mr. Silver was really impressed."

"That so?"

"Yessiree and now he's interested in you participating in a race he's organizing…"

"Will it be dangerous?" Samson asked.

"Yes," Enzo replied simply.

Samson said, "I'll do it."

Enzo clapped his hands once. "Fabulous!"

That night Samson had a dream he was being chased by thousands of snakes. Or were they vines? He couldn't really tell. The dream ended as he was devoured in the midst of an oceanic whirlpool while the sound of a car engine shook him to the core.

V.

Behind the finish line was the stadium seating filled to the brim with wild spectators screaming for their favorite racer. Some were wearing transparent plastic skull masks in honor of Drac. Others wore yellow shirts with the name SAMSON emblazoned across the front in bold, black letters.

Samson had the gas pedal down to the floor. His hands gripped the wheel so hard he felt his knuckles burn. Paulo was still crouched down on the floor of the passenger side, biting his fingernails. Drac was ahead of them by five feet, his glass skull shining in the sun.

"Go, goddamnit, go," Samson said, talking to his car. Paulo looked at him with visible hurt on his face. "I wasn't talking to you, kid. Just the car."

Then he shook his head as he watched Drac speed through the finish line, cutting the ribbon in half, a piece of it falling on Samson's windshield to mark his complete and utter failure.

CHAPTER TWENTY

Yowzah! Yowzah! Yowzah! We have a winner!

Can you believe it? Drac Dunwich, Mr. Glass Skull himself, has won the race! Poor old Samson, he's the loser but let's face it, he's given us great entertainment, right? Well, maybe not as much as Mr. Dunwich but hey, we all can't be show-stoppers!

Now let's get ready for Mr. Silver. Yep, you heard me right. Mr. Silver is coming out to personally congratulate the winner. We'll also see the bonus prize handed off to Drac for killing Lord Bing Bong. Is everybody excited? Hell yeah!

I.

Drac drove through the gate, past the finish line and onto a ramp that brought him onto the boardwalk. A large crescent-shaped stadium had been built on the boardwalk and the beach, giving Drac a view of the audience that had been watching the entire race. What shocked him was not the cacophony of cheers but the sight of people wearing masks that looked like him. Should he have been flattered? He wasn't.

After driving up onto the boardwalk, he stopped at the

stage that had been built over the beach. Standing on top of that stage was Enzo in his tacky white suit and behind him, a tall man with a ponytail. His grin cut his face in half, revealing bright yellow teeth.

Drac stepped out of the car to the ear-crushing din of the audience. He slammed the car door and looked over the stage to the ocean where the city of R'lyeh was waiting like a wrapped present he was about to be forced to open. A green stone bridge had been built from the stage to R'lyeh, crossing the water like a witch's finger directing him to his fate.

He turned around and saw Samson pull up. How was the guy going to accept defeat? Was he going to jump out and accuse Drac of cheating? Would he just get out and shoot him?

Drac stared through the windshield of Samson's car and saw that he wasn't making a move to get out. Samson stared back at him.

The loudspeakers blared. "Congratulations, Drac Dunwich! Yowzah!"

The crowd cheered and Drac looked up to large video screens hanging on the sides of several hotels. He looked at his face, his glass skull, his brain soaked in gasoline...

"Yowzah! Let me turn things over to the boss. Yes, Mr. Silver himself!"

Enzo handed the microphone to Silver, who smiled even wider. He laughed and the chuckling reverberated down the boardwalk. It was so loud that Drac expected the hotels to tremble.

"Well, well, there's my winner. There's my Drac Dunwich. I should have known the driver wearing the Halloween costume would win the death race."

Enzo laughed. It made a hollow sound that chilled Drac's

spine.

Silver went on. "Now, before we get to anything else, let's talk about your bonus prize for killing Lord Bing Bong. You really took a thorn out of my side and I appreciate it. Oh, do I appreciate it. And because I do, I'm going to award you with something I know you'll enjoy." He made a gesture to someone behind Drac.

From behind him walked Mr. Silver's "enforcer", the man called COP, in a leather mask and codpiece, with eyes that were a milky hell. On his shoulders he carried a large cube of green flesh. He dropped it at Drac's feet and said, "Food."

The crowd laughed.

Silver whistled into the microphone. "Whew, yessir, Drac. You got yourself a nice-looking cube of Yugg meat. Cop there, he was half right. You could use it as food, of course, but there are so many other uses. Smoke it, snort it, do your laundry with it. I've heard you can bind books with it, too. So put that into your car and let me go on about your…prize." Silver laughed, turning to Enzo who snickered into his palm. That was all Lord Bing Bong's life was worth: a cube of Yugg meat. They found it hilarious.

Drac heard a car door slam. Samson had gotten out of his car and was walking next to him.

"Congratulations," Samson said.

Drac nodded.

They both looked at the stage as Mr. Silver smirked. He said, "What I like about being an entertainer is that I have the freedom to…change things as I see fit. I call it the Berlusconi rule of power. I mean, you two men participated in the race of your lives and it entertained the crowd. But it's not as simple as that." He snapped his fingers and Cop walked to Samson's car, opened the passenger door, and pulled Paulo out by the neck.

"Hey, you get the hell away from him!" Samson said, running over. Cop punched him squarely in the nose. He fell to the ground, blinded by tears and pain. But through the tears he watched Cop drag Paulo up to the stage where Mr. Silver grabbed the boy's neck, holding him in place.

Cop walked back to Samson, grabbed a handful of hair, and dragged him to the front of the stage where he stayed on his knees, looking up at Paulo, Mr. Silver, and Enzo.

Mr. Silver put the microphone to his mouth and blew into it, causing a wave of static to erupt from the speakers. Then he said, "Samson. You're courageous, chivalrous and stoic. You saved this boy from an uncertain fate, right? Well, I never said you could have a partner in the race, now did I?"

"He wasn't a partner," Samson said.

"Oh, well, I guess…" Silver started but was interrupted by Enzo.

"Mr. Silver, sir, may I have a word with you?" he said. "In private?"

Silver nodded and dropped the mic to the ground. He threw Paulo to the ground and bent his head down so Enzo could whisper into his ear.

"There is something strange about the boy."

"What do you mean?"

"I feel something," Enzo said. "I feel something ancient under the surface of his skin. Something to do with power. Something to do with…that." He pointed out to the sea, towards R'lyeh.

"You mean…."

"He is not a real child," Enzo said. "He's…."

Silver nodded in understanding and walked back to the

end of the stage and picked up the microphone. He motioned for Enzo to grab hold of Paulo. Then he looked at Samson. "You've come to value this...boy, right?"

Samson didn't respond. Cop kicked him in the ribs and said, "Answer."

Samson shook his head which brought on another kick and another. Finally he said, "Right."

Silver said, "He was such a fragile child, in need of rescue and you swooped in like a hero and rescued him. Now look at him." He moved Paulo around by the neck, to the right and then to the left. The boy didn't struggle with the hand grabbing his neck. He looked catatonic.

"Well, Samson, this is sort of...ironic...considering your history."

"What are you talking about?" Samson lifted himself to his feet.

"I'm talking about...Jack."

Samson's heart sank. During the race, he had tried his best to bury his memories about his son. Having a young boy in the passenger seat actually helped him do that, as if the presence of Paulo had taken the place of the past. But now...

"What the hell are you talking about?" he said, tensing to jump up on stage and tear Silver apart.

"Samson, I'm talking about the son you failed to save. You see, I'm a businessman. That's it. Not only do I deal in consumer goods but in information, knowledge. I know many things, Samson. Rarely does something happen in New Jersey that I don't know about or approve."

Silver dug his fingers into Paulo's neck, tearing flesh. The crowd was silent except for a few random gasps.

Samson jumped forward but was held back by Cop. The

smell of fish filled his nostrils as the brute gripped him like a vise. "What the fuck are you doing!" he yelled at Silver.

Silver tilted his head and smiled. "I'm opening a book."

II.

When Silver started tearing out the kid's flesh, Drac almost pissed his pants. He'd seen some fucked-up stuff before but nothing like this. It's one thing if a racer ran over a kid during the race. That was a violent moment of adrenaline that could be understood if not excused. But to mutilate a young boy in front of a crowd of people? That was absurdly unnecessary.

He crossed his arms and watched as Silver continued to strip off the skin from the boy, tearing muscle until he was grabbing handfuls of something that didn't look like it belonged in a human body.

With a sinister smile on his face, Mr. Silver was pulling page after yellowed page of parchment out of Paulo's mangled body. The boy was not real, was not a living child.

The kid had been a living, breathing accursed tome.

Samson let out a howl of anguish and confusion and watched as Paulo was torn up, his flesh thrown aside while paper was pulled from his shell-like body.

Drac just stood and watched silently.

Silver tore a handful of pages out from under Paulo's ribcage and the body, now emptied, dropped to the ground.

"Don't you worry, Samson," Silver said. "The kid was never real. Well, at least not as real as your son."

III.

Two Weeks Ago

Simon Revair held the *Abgrund Abschaum* and smiled.

Finally, he possessed it: the harbinger of the new age. He put the book to his nose and inhaled the scent of primordial knowledge, leathery flesh, and the skin cells of ancient fingers.

Simon put the book on the engine and got into the car to start it.

The revving of the engine warmed the tome. Simon dug into the trunk and brought out his supplies: four buckets of clay and a bag of tools made of bone and metal. He walked over to the engine and stared down at the book, watching flakes of parchment flutter up into his face. He inhaled them.

Then he got to work.

It took him four hours but when he was done, he had transformed the *Abgrund Abschaum* into a walking herald of oblivion, a book in the form of a child.

"Wake up," he said to the small form below him.

The child-thing stirred and sat up. It looked at Simon and said, "I'm awake."

"That you are, my son. That you are.

IV.

Silver looked at Drac and winked. "Don't worry. I didn't forget about you."

"What? What's the point of all this?" Drac said.

"Straight to the point. I like that. Let me tell you. You two men are so special to me, to all of us." Silver motioned to the crowd, giving them permission to cheer. "You are two top-notch entertainers and now you'll have the chance to entertain us even more."

Drac said, "The race is done."

"Oh, is it? No, I don't think it is. See that bridge?" Silver pointed to the green bridge that had been constructed to stretch all the way to the city of R'lyeh. "You two will be racing over it."

Samson grunted. "The hell I will."

Drac concurred. "I don't see a reason why I need to race again. I already won."

The audience erupted in hoots and howls. How dare the two racers deny Mr. Silver?

"Boys, you don't seem to understand. You both are going over that bridge. There's no discussion. Samson, I'm sure you're wondering how I know about Jack and I'll only say this. When you go over that bridge, you'll be entering a whole new realm of truth, of reality. Granted, it may not be the reality you want to face but, well, it's the reality that's waiting for you." Silver grinned. "Jack's waiting for you."

Samson's heart dropped. He looked over at the city. It was a bulbous, gargantuan island that rose from the sea like a monstrous pimple. It pulsed and throbbed like an oceanic heart sending ominous sound waves into Samson's ears. It was strange that it hadn't appeared in his peripheral vision. It was as if it only existed if he viewed it with undivided attention. The chlorochrous city walls ended at impossible angles. He rubbed his eyes in fear that he was hallucinating. The walls were decorated with holocryptic symbols. Beyond the walls there were spiraling obelisks and monolithic slabs of cock-eyed rock that reached up to the clouds.

And now to think Jack might be within those walls.

Silver's voice interrupted his mediation. "It looks magnificent, doesn't it? Almost makes you glad all the modern cities have been destroyed. They were all fucking garbage anyway. Trash heaps full of worthless meat."

Drac shouted. "What makes you think I'll race again?"

Silver said nothing. He stepped over the scraps of Paulo on the stage and stood on the edge. "Because....."

Drac felt a crack and saw a flash. He brought his hand to the back of his glass skull and felt a small gash. Then he fell into a laughing, black abyss.

V.

Samson heard Drac hit the ground. Another hulking thug similar to Cop stood behind him holding a club with small spikes protruding out of it. This guy was identical to Cop except that on his chest was written the word SLAVE.

Silver spoke again, this time his voice sounding less amused and more intense. He took a few steps off the stage and stood close to Samson.

"You're going to get into your car and you're going to race across the bridge to the city...to Jack."

Samson trembled with adrenalin. There was so much anger it actually calmed him, covered his body and mind with a blanket of focused intensity. Everything had led to this, his one chance of finding Jack. Tomato Joe had mentioned Silver and how he bought people. But could that scumbag biker be trusted? Was Silver just playing with him? Regardless, he had to find out.

Samson stood watching as Cop and Slave put Drac into his car. They pushed it up onto the bridge. Then they turned around and stared at Samson, their milky eyes glowing.

"Fine," Samson said. "I'll race." He got into his car.

Silver smiled widely, his voice becoming cheerful again. "Okay then. Let's get this show on the road...."

He was interrupted by the roar of the crowd and for a minute, Mr. Silver thought it was simply because of the announcement, but then he heard shouts of surprise from the stands.

"Oh my god!" someone yelled. "It's Gabby!"

CHAPTER TWENTY-ONE

Didja hear that, folks? Gabby's back!
Yowzah!

*

Mr. Silver smiled as Gabby clawed her way out of the huge hunk of Yugg meat he had awarded Drac.

It had been such an ingenious plan to sew that crazy bitch back together, a shame it had taken so much valuable Yugg meat. The look on their faces was priceless, that look of shock and awe.

Gabby crawled out of the gooey cube of flesh. Her limbs were twisted like misshapen tree roots, her nude body covered in dark green moss and gaping holes that oozed black goo. She pulled her hammer out from between her legs and her cell phone from her ass cheeks. One hand held the phone to her ear while the other waved the hammer in the air. She ran over to the crowd and made quick work of the spectators.

"Cha-cha-cha-cha-cha-cha-cha-cha-chat!" she muttered through broken lips into the cell phone while using her pink hammer to attack the crowd indiscriminately. Young women were beaten to a pulp, their breasts crushed, ripped off, and thrown into the air. The skulls of children were bashed in until brains flew into the air like wet popcorn. Several men had the pleasure of the pink hammer slamming into their scrotum, popping their testicles into oblivion.

Silver nodded in approval, loving the spectacle of it all. He looked at Samson who was staring at his hands as they gripped the steering wheel. Silver scoffed. Some people just didn't appreciate good entertainment.

After a few dozen people were slaughtered, he turned to his forces. "Okay, you can get that cunt out of here now," he said to Cop and Slave. The two hulking thugs ran over to the audience.

Just as they got to her, Gabby ran down the stands, tripping over several spectators who did nothing but watch the bloody entertainment. The two hulks stomped through the crowd, following Gabby and finally getting a hold of her at the bottom of the bleachers.

Cop grabbed Gabby's shoulders, his fingers digging into the gaping holes. Slave grabbed her waist and squeezed. The top half of Gabby's body fell to the ground and pulled itself from Cop's grip. It started to crawl away while the bottom half kicked at Slave.

"Gabby! Gabby! Gabby!" the crowd cheered and dozens of people pushed Cop and Slave aside. They started stomping both pieces of Gabby into mossy pulp in a frenzy of elation.

CHAPTER TWENTY-TWO

Well, gang, you saw it for yourself. Not only did you get a hell of a race but you were witness to Gabby's violent return and her second violent demise. Wow!

And not only that…but we have a second race ahead of us! Sure, Drac had to be, uh, persuaded but he's been strapped into his car and the engine's revved up. He'll be waking up any second. And look at Samson there, I haven't seen him so intense since the race started. This is going to be one hell of a show!

I.

Drac woke up with his hands gripping the steering wheel. What the hell happened? He remembered looking up at Silver and then….

Pain pierced the back of his glass skull. Yeah, he remembered. Someone must have sucker punched him.

He looked through the windshield at R'lyeh and shuddered.

Streams of memories flooded through his mind. Intricately drawn blueprints in a rotting book. Words of an unknown language carved into stone. Ancient machines pumping gasoline into his body. An atrous sky falling. A cascade of tentacles.

Millions of tentacles.

He felt a sinister familiarity. Hadn't his father mentioned a city like this once? Didn't he say a man couldn't gaze upon it without going insane?

Drac was no stranger to the preternatural but the very sight of the city made his bowels ache in fearful anticipation. This was no ordinary city of ancient times. This was no quaint Atlantis or beautifully obscure Carcosa. This was a city that was carved from horror itself, a pulsating totem to an ultra-terrestrial civilization.

From outside he heard Silver's voice blaring, "Get ready, drivers!"

In the rearview mirror he saw the boardwalk, the audience standing on their seats, and Silver's face on five giant video screens. Drac went to put his car in reverse but felt a rumbling.

The part of the bridge behind him was collapsing into the water.

Silver's voice sounded again. "You better get going, gentlemen. The bridge is taking part in the race, too!"

Drac quickly looked over at Samson whose car was right next to him. The two men's eyes met for a split second, silently acknowledging that they both had to get the hell out of there.

They sped off down the bridge.

II.

As he drove down the green bridge alongside Drac, Samson

looked into his rearview mirror and saw the bridge collapsing behind him in a cloud of emerald dust, green rubble cascading into the sea. There was nowhere to go but forward, no turning away from this mysterious city.

The bridge seemed to go on forever and the city of R'lyeh wasn't getting any closer. Samson looked at Drac, expecting to see some guns drawn or some other threat but was surprised to see the glass-skulled racer looking straight ahead as if in a trance. Maybe the guy had made the same decision as Samson. He was simply going to go forward with the expectation of a violent, bizarre death. There was no other outcome. Silver had made sure of it. How foolish they both were to expect any different.

There were no happy endings.

But what about Jack?

Had Silver bought him? Was Tomato Joe just one of Silver's tools for domination? Maybe he went around stealing kids for his own amusement, for entertainment.

Samson knew he was a fool to believe Silver was going to give him the opportunity to find out the truth about Jack. That wasn't the type of game Silver played. But maybe, just maybe…

He looked into the sky above R'lyeh, wanting so much to see Jack's face up in the clouds, evidence the boy was in some sort of heaven. The city seemed to rise up higher and block his view of the clouds. Samson could see now that Silver had placed some of his troops on the walls of the city. The troops were dressed in bright yellow armor, pre-war police uniforms. Demonic masks covered the faces of every soldier, reminding Samson of golden gargoyles.

He thought about creeping in behind Drac, letting the other guy take the risk of being first within the city walls. But the crumbling bridge was too close behind them, Samson couldn't do it. They had to go in together.

They were a quarter mile away from the city when Samson saw the dark crimson light at the entrance, glowing in between two monstrous sigils engraved on the wall. The light opened like an incarnadine anus, expanding until the wall was replaced by an orifice large enough for the two cars to pass through.

As they approached, Samson thought about driving off the bridge and into the water. Maybe he could swim somewhere safe, forget about the goddamn race. He could start a new life somewhere, find an uncontaminated beach, and just live.

Or maybe he could just drown himself, finally give himself up to fate, to death, to whatever unknown is waiting out there.

But what if Silver wasn't lying? What if the truth about Jack was somewhere in the city?

Side by side with Drac, Samson entered the city of R'lyeh, a thick, reddish darkness enveloping them. They were sucked into the crimson light.

III.

When they entered the city, Drac took his foot off the gas pedal and coasted his way inside. He hadn't expected there to be such darkness. It was as if there was a roof over their heads where there couldn't have been. Drac looked to the sky but instead of clouds, there were inky shadows, like jellied smoke.

He engaged his car's tentacles to act as feelers but they weren't working. Had Silver messed with his car when Drac was asleep?

The headlights of the cars didn't do much to disperse the blackness so both Drac and Samson coasted slowly, now realizing that anything could be waiting for them. Where were they supposed to go?

Drac didn't know.

So he just kept driving into the black.

IV.

There were roads now. Samson hadn't really expected there to be, considering the city was supposedly built before mankind even had use for roads. They drove down a wide even street that ran between massive insectoid skyscrapers.

The road itself was made of smooth, glistening obsidian. The buildings were rocking back and forth, squirming and quivering like monolithic tongues. Gaping holes in the buildings puffed clouds of yellow mist, spreading out like sinister parachutes.

As if made of clay, the buildings began to melt into bizarre shapes, hanging over the road like sinister tree branches. Samson sped as fast as he could, worried the buildings might drop right down on him.

Drac was right behind him, swerving now as if dodging invisible obstacles.

A rush of sound erupted from Samson's right and he grabbed his ear in pain. A hole in one of the buildings had erupted with tiny flying things, things too small for Samson to identify. He could hear them biting at his car, scraping the paint off.

Some of the things crashed into his windshield and he put his face close to the glass. They were tiny octopoid creatures with wings. Their tentacles frantically kicked at the glass.

Some of the creatures flew in through the back of his car where the back window used to be. One flew around Samson's head, landing on his nose, sticking its tentacles in his nostrils, intertwining with his nose hairs.

"Goddamn!" he swatted at the thing, crushing it against his skin, its body popped into a gooey stain. He sent his fists around the car, grabbing the creatures and squeezing until they burst. Soon the remainder of them left the way they came and went back to attacking the front of the car.

Samson turned on the windshield wipers, slaughtering dozens.

There was an explosion behind him that rocked his car. In the rearview he saw a fireball growing behind Drac's car.

"Shit," he said, as he drove on, wanting to avoid catching fire or being rammed by Drac. Up ahead there was a cathedral-like building constructed out of glass, machine parts, and elephantine intestines.

The machine parts were like nothing Samson had ever seen: misshapen gear-like things turned at obscure angles, twisting into shapes and forming the spires of the cathedral. Black holes formed and disappeared on the brick walls while green metal spears jutted out and were quickly sucked back like serpent's tongues.

A figure cloaked in a yellow robe stood in front of the cathedral. Samson turned just in time, barely missing the figure but glimpsing the thing's face. It looked like the underside of a horseshoe crab with glistening segmented appendages that wiggled obscenely.

Drac was right behind him as Samson sped down another street, this one with buildings made entirely of red crystal. He could see there were things encased within the crystal, like insects in amber. But these weren't insects.

They looked humanoid except they had red and white tentacles instead of heads. As Samson drove by, each of these things started to move through the crystal. He grabbed his gun but realized it would probably be useless against all of them at once.

Drac pulled up along side him, his arm out the window, shooting at the tentacle-head things that were now crawling out of their homes and leaping onto the street like angry gorillas. Samson drove straight into one, flipping it over the car. He looked into the rearview mirror and saw it splatter on the road.

He brought his gun up and shot out the window at some of the things. They jumped onto his car. Samson swerved back and forth, one of them reached into the car, wrapping its head-tentacles around his neck.

"Jesus Christ!" he said, pistol-whipping the slimy hands of the creature. Its tentacle reached into the car and slithered between Samson's legs. It caressed his crotch and then shot down to his feet, pushing down the brake pedal.

The car skidded but Samson turned the wheel to the right, whipping the creature off the car and into the path of Drac who ran into it, decorating the street with gore.

Samson lost some headway but he stepped on the gas and followed Drac down the road, shooting at the creatures who dared to get near either car.

At the end of the street there was another cathedral, this one a gigantic mass of sludge and vegetation. Samson saw there was nowhere to go but into the building. Its huge sigil-covered doors opened and he followed Drac into the darkness of the chthonic temple.

V.

The sound of chattering teeth.

That's all Samson heard. The roar of his engine was no match for the noise of whatever waited in the darkness. Next to him he could make out the faint interior light of Drac's car which illuminated the guy's glass skull, making it appear as if it floated there in the car separate from his body.

Up ahead there was a flash of iridescent light. Samson slowed down and swerved to the left, knowing he might very well end up in some hole or trap. Instead, he ran something over, something that crunched under his tires. Something slammed into the right side of his car. It was Drac, trying to avoid the same green flash.

"Watch yourself," Samson said, pretending for a moment that the other driver could hear him.

The green flash grew into a door, a gaping hole that led them into a chamber constructed out of lizard skin. In the chamber were a seemingly infinite number of floating spheres. Samson and Drac drove straight into them.

The spheres bombarded the two cars, cracking glass and splattering unearthly goo. It was like driving in a rainstorm, if the raindrops were huge and glowing, quivering into different forms. The spheres turned into things Samson could not comprehend, could never describe.

Ahead of him the cascade of sphere-things pulled apart like a curtain, putting a hole in the lizard-skin room and Samson found himself driving straight into a courtyard full of...

VI.

Flowers.

It was a shocking juxtaposition, driving from a spooky spherical abyss to a courtyard of light and flowers. Drac kept trying to get his tentacles to work and finally they listened to him, coming out from underneath his car like reluctant kittens. Drac tried getting them to feel things out in front of him but it was no use. After a few seconds, they drooped. It was as if the city itself was sucking the energy from the tendrils, making them nothing but flaccid appendages.

"What the hell?" he said, his jaw dropping in glassy shock. In the center of the courtyard stood a large stone slab, bearing a gigantic flower made of flesh and feces that shimmered with a brunneous glow.

The courtyard itself seemed infinite. The sky, a crisp blue, was barely visible above as thick, ugly clouds flooded in quickly. In addition to the fecal-flower, there were hundreds of other organisms Drac could not identify. Flowers with flat tendrils instead of leaves, throbbing thorns leaking neon poison, gaping mouths filled with more gaping mouths, leafy blobs hanging from obsidian obelisks.

Drac and Samson kept driving through the bizarre foliage, their cars tearing fishy vines and smashing through jellyfish stalks. Oceanic gore splattered their windshields. The moldy floor of the courtyard slowed them down and as they kept driving, they felt like they were losing ground instead of gaining it.

From out of the stone slab came a plethora of black tentacles. They grabbed onto Drac's car and wrapped around it like a greedy child holding a treasured toy.

"Son of a bitch!" Drac yelled, trying to gain focus, trying to turn the situation to his advantage. He was being overpowered by tentacles while his own were impotent. He swerved the car, trying to get it out of the monstrous grasp.

Samson's car had already swerved away to avoid being a target, but the moldy ground made his car swerve, swinging in a circle until it was facing Drac's car.

The convertible top was pulled off Drac's car and a tentacle dove into the backseat, tearing into the bottom of the car. Then it stopped.

Drac grabbed his gun fired at the tentacles but then realized Samson's car was right alongside him again with the blowgun on top firing away.

Samson was helping him.

VII.

Samson didn't give a shit about the race. He saw the tentacles attack Drac and the move to help him was instinctual. He wondered if that's how it felt to be in combat alongside someone you didn't like. They had a common enemy in Silver, the man who had put them in this abominable place, why shouldn't they team up?

He navigated his vehicle so he was right up close to Drac and then used his blowgun on the tentacles. There was no way of knowing if the needles would have any effect on them but it was worth a try. They weren't giving up. Drac's car was being torn to shreds.

Samson decided to take a chance and try something risky. He let go of the blowgun trigger and leaned over to open the passenger door with his right hand while steering the car with his left. He was hoping Drac would see him and know what he intended to do.

Drac's glass skull turned and his eyes met Samson's. Then Drac grabbed his large, white gun.

VIII.

Drac fired.

The tentacles shook at every blast, still holding on but giving him just the few seconds he needed to get a grip on his car and jump over to Samson's.

It wasn't an easy task. Drac's spiked shoulder pads and purple cape made it quite difficult to safely jump from one moving car to another.

But Drac did it.

He surprised himself. The top half of his body fell right onto Samson's passenger seat and his right hand gripped the open door. His legs dangled, scraping the ground, sending up bulbous spores that crackled in the air.

Samson hooked his arm under Drac's and started to pull him in. A tentacle wrapped around Drac's feet, squeezing his thighs until he screamed in high-pitched agony.

A blast from Samson's gun blew the tentacle apart, allowing Drac to pull himself up into the car.

"Holy shit." Drac didn't know what else to say. The rescue had been unexpected.

"Yeah," Samson said. "You got that gun, you should use it."

Drac hadn't realized he still had the gun in his hand. He put his arm out the window and fired at the tentacles that were waving in their direction. He watched his car veer off to the right and crash into a pile of red, bulbous skulls that screamed on impact.

Samson maneuvered the car away from the tentacles, circling around other strange looking plant life toward an exit underneath a stone arch made of green stone, into more darkness. The windshield fogged up and the headlights of the car did nothing to penetrate the black.

As they drove through the nothingness, Drac said, "Thank you."

Samson nodded. "So what now?"

"I don't know," Drac said. "I doubt we'll get out of here alive."

"Yeah."

Drac looked around at the dashboard and then started to run his hands across it while Samson steered blindly.

Finally, Samson said, "You looking for something?"

"What do you mean?"

"You're rubbing the car like it's a woman."

Drac quickly took his hands away but was still looking at the dashboard with his eyes wide open. "There's something familiar about this car. I don't know what it is. I just feel like I've seen it before."

"Yeah?"

"Where'd you get it?"

Samson turned the steering wheel right, seeing if perhaps there was a path out of the darkness. But there wasn't.

He said, "It's a long story."

"So?"

Samson said, "Got it from a guy in Dogunville."

"A guy?"

"Yeah."

Drac slowly extended his arm and put his hand on the steering wheel next to Samson's. He said, "Who was he?"

"I don't know. Some guy."

"What was his name?" Drac said, his high-pitched voice turning deep, guttural.

Samson tensed up, thinking it was a mistake for him to have rescued the guy but then he realized Drac's aggressiveness had nothing to do with him. "I think it was Simon..."

"Simon *what?*"

"Simon...Revair, I think."

Drac took his hand off the wheel and put it to his skull. The gasoline inside him percolated, stirring up atoms of memory.

IX.

There was a cut on Drac's leg. It was a bad one. Samson remembered when his Jack was very young, that when he was hurt he would run into Samson's arms and say, "Daddy, I got a boo-boo!" Samson would kiss it, tell Jack he would be okay, and watch the pain disappear from the boy's face.

He wondered if Drac's father did the same thing. Thinking of that strange glass-skulled man as a child filled Samson with warm empathy and he was tempted to ask Drac about his father.

But there was no time for that.

The only thing Samson could think about was Jack. He had wandered aimlessly for years, searching for the boy, thinking about where he was, what had happened to him. If he was alive, he couldn't be in a place like this, no human could survive in a place like this for long.

Samson glanced over at Drac. He was deep in thought, his eyes glazed over and his hands trembled on his lap. The death race had taken its toll on both men.

Who exactly was this Simon Revair whose name made Drac respond with such horror? Samson remembered him vaguely; even the memory of receiving the car seemed to be made of the same thing as dreams. Revair's face changed in his mind, dropping off like a loose mask as another took its place. Samson realized he would not be able to pick the man out of a crowd. The memory had been contaminated by time and perhaps…something else.

X.

Ten Years Ago

The Church of the Starry Engines always held their meetings in a disused storefront, an anonymous room with wooden tables and wicker chairs. Maps, both new and old, covered two of the walls while primordial sigils were scrawled on the others. Constellations of mud and scum covered the ceiling.

The congregation settled in, sitting in the chairs and on the floor which was stained with motor oil, antifreeze, gasoline, and blood. The whole room stank of machine rituals and primeval combustion.

An oil-slicked prism sat in the center of the room, emitting pulses of energy that filled each member of the congregation with dread and trepidation. But they did not mind. In fact, they wouldn't have it any other way.

A handsome man with bright blue eyes stepped out from a shadowy corner. He had been there the whole time, biding his time, meditating on the future of his group, of his church, of his people. His heart revved like an engine, his mind became a turbine of ancient power. Through his veins flowed the blood of a thousand mechanical horrors, ageless and brewing with hatred for the human race that had infested the earth like fragile insects.

The man walked up to the prism, stuck out his quivering tongue, and licked the fluids off. He stared into the crystal, saw countless years of fallen stars being constructed into automotive blasphemies, and fell into a trance.

He chanted and the congregation chanted with him.

He raised his hands and the congregation raised theirs.

This man, Simon Revair, pastor of the church, took hold of the prism and held it above his head. He instructed a member of the congregation to get the tools. It was time to get to work.

It was time to reconstruct the ancient machine which would raise its home from the depths of the sea. It would take a decade and there was much more to do but it would be worth it.

Simon Revair sighed in ecstasy. Oh yes, it would be worth it.

XI.

"What's wrong?" Samson said.

"I don't know. Something doesn't feel...right," Drac said, holding his arms down, feeling the vibration of the engine and looking out into the darkness.

Then: light.

It came instantly, an abrupt flash of yellow that brought

them into the sunlight. They drove into a walled enclosure at least three square miles, with looping stone roads rising and falling like a holographic puzzle.

There were a myriad of roads to choose from but it didn't seem to matter. Samson couldn't see any way out. As his eyes followed one of the roads that rose to the sky, he saw that it ended in a spiral. It was a corkscrew horror covered in a group of winged creatures that looked like flying lobsters.

There were other flying things. Orbs that were like black suns made of meat. Crab-like triangles with thin, pink tentacles. Headless faces floating around blobs of smoke.

Drac groaned. "Something's wrong."

"Yeah, I know. Look at those things."

"No, I don't mean that. I mean....."

Samson looked over at Drac who was staring down at himself. Something *was* wrong. Drac's arms had started to melt into the car seat, his skin melding with it.

"Holy shit," Samson said, as he drove the car up one ramp and onto a stone road that twisted into unbelievable angles. He felt his hands tingle and saw the flesh on his fingers drop and become one with the leather steering wheel. "Goddamnit."

He tried to take his hands off the wheel but they wouldn't move.

He tried to take his foot off the gas pedal but it wouldn't move.

"What the hell?"

"Just keep driving."

Though he could feel the car's speed and see the speedometer reach its limit, Samson saw none of the surroundings move in the appropriate way. Everything stood still, every crystallized spiral, every fleshy black sun, every winged terror. They all stood as still as a snapshot while the car's engine roared forward, its wheels burning rubber on the cold, green stone beneath it. The road was bringing them somewhere.

Samson's eyes searched the surrounding area and saw it: a door made of metallic hairs.

The road brought them through it. Sparks fell onto the windshield, burning through the glass and bubbling onto the dashboard. The road had brought them into a gigantic dome-shaped chamber. Samson thought that it was impossible. From the outside, the city hadn't looked tall enough to harbor such a place. But there they were, driving up a spiraling stone road toward the ceiling which grew farther and farther away no matter how fast they seemed to be going in its direction.

The dome ceiling split open like a gangrenous wound and revealed a labyrinth of machinery constructed out of stone and giant crustaceans.

Hundreds of emaciated human bodies hung from the machinery. From the neck down their flesh had been stripped from their bodies. Only their faces revealed the person they had been prior to their torture. Samson searched the faces of the damned. Their expressions were purposeless. They were just empty shells, decorations. Their skin was greased with motor oil which dripped from their feet like slow, dark rain.

Samson felt his skin loosen from his body. He was becoming just one more instrument of the car. His bones melded with metal. His veins expanded into tubes and pipes and his skin became leather upholstery.

The car sped toward a group of human bodies and Samson saw the face he had been thinking about for years.

Jack's face.

His son was older, yes, but it was him. His skin had been

flayed but it was him, Samson was sure of it. He let out a groan.

Drac said, "What is it?"

"My son."

"It's not your son. Those are just bodies."

"It's him!"

Drac scoffed.

With all his strength, Samson steered the car in the direction of Jack's body. The road wasn't going to bring him close enough, Samson was going to have to drive off the road and into the air.

Drac said, "What the hell are you doing?"

"I'm going to get my son."

"You're going to kill us!"

"What the hell are you talking about? What do you think is going to happen to us?"

"That's not your son! Not anymore!"

Samson pressed his foot down on the pedal, taking advantage of the fact that he was part of the car now. The tires started to rumble and as Samson looked out of the windshield toward his son, he saw something else.

Behind the flayed bodies was a monstrous creature made of wet, green flesh and a grotesque shell. Dozens of wings protruded from its body while two giant orbs served as eyes that stared out at Samson and Drac with ungodly ambivalence.

The monstrous creature let out a breath and the flayed bodies began to sway back and forth until their fluids battered Samson's car in a torrential downpour of blood and oil.

The giant orbs blinked. Wings fluttered and bodies started to fall.

In horror, Samson saw Jack's near lifeless body fall to the

road in front of him and steered the car into it. If he could just get him to land on the hood...

For a second he saw Jack's eyes looking at him. Could it be possible he recognized his father? It seemed that way or at least that's what Samson hoped. The body crashed into the car and through the windshield. There was a shower of glass and blood.

Jack landed in the car, the top half of his body lying in the backseat with the lower in the front. With an inhuman groan, the body pulled itself to the front.

Jack's face was weathered and pockmarked from years of exposure to cosmic horrors. His flayed body exposed not only his bloody flesh but also tiny stone insects embedded in the muscle and fat. Jack bared his teeth which were stained with ancient seaweed ink and his tongue oozed out of his mouth: a pink tentacle covered with inhuman taste buds.

Samson could only move his eyes enough to see a small bit of his son's face, not the face of a boy he lost but had never forgotten, a man's face, a man spending eternity in an incomprehensible hell.

Through tears he said, "Son."

A shriek escaped from Jack, emanating not from his throat but from the stone insects. Then a guttural cough from Jack's mouth sounded to Samson like, "Dad."

Tears of salty motor oil flowed from Samson's eyes. "I'm sorry, Jack."

XII.

Drac listened to the exchange between Samson and the flayed body and felt jealousy.

His own father was an intelligent man but lacked the devotion and kindness that was evident in Samson. Drac doubted his father would have had the same emotional pull towards his son.

Before him appeared a circular shell, immense in size and sparkling with colors unknown to any earthly rainbow. Images flickered on the shell like cryptic runes on a primordial television. Drac saw his father sitting at an ornate wooden table, a book opened in front of him. A young man sat down at the table. At first Drac thought the young man was him but then quickly realized it was not. It was Simon Revair.

A black envelope emerged from of the book and was taken by Revair who opened it and pulled out a photograph. His mouth gaped and his eyes widened. Drac's father then closed the book, stood up, and patted Revair on the shoulder.

Drac tried to close his eyes to the images on the shell but couldn't. He watched his father offer him, his firstborn son, to the Church of Starry Engines. Gasoline tears started to pump out of his eyes. The roar of the car's engine invaded his skull and brought pain and memory. He thought of his father and cursed the man for his betrayal, for his devotion not to his son but to his research and his church.

All of the images faded and Drac was left looking out at the gargantuan beast staring down at him as the car sped upward into an empyreal abyss.

XIII.

There was no sky left, just crab shell clouds and that giant beast staring them down, its moist skin oozing octopoid sweat that flew down like hungry hail, smashing into the car, peppering it with holes.

That's when the road cleared. With a groan that sounded as ancient as it was ear-destroying, the creature flew out of sight and Samson saw that they were now heading straight toward a translucent wall covered with throbbing suckers and tentacles made of quivering mirrors.

And they went right through that wall, a multiverse of tentacles engulfing the car.

Jack pulled himself up onto his father's lap, alien sounds erupting from every remaining cell of his body. He started to melt.

Samson tried moving his hands off the steering wheel to hug his son but he was still just part of the car, just another instrument in a biomechanical horror. But he felt Jack's body soften and meld into his own. They were together and would be forever, that was better than nothing.

"I love you, Jack," he said, trying to determine if his son's consciousness was going to be a part of him as well as his body.

What Samson was headed toward had nothing to do with a death race. It was beyond life and death, beyond anything that anyone on earth could have ever imagined.

As Jack's and his body became more machine than human, he drove into an abyss of unimaginable horror and Samson realized he'd be there forever. No roads. No light. No cities. No earth. No sky.

Samson let tears gush out in a bitter deluge of motor oil.

EPILOGUE

Mr. Silver snickered.

Everything had gone exactly as planned, better, even. It was the spectacle of the thing that was important. It was the pomp, the glitz, the sheer entertainment value that filled him with power.

He had been having the dreams since he was a child but up until recently he had not known the meaning of them. He had believed them to be bizarre, childish fantasies taking place in some fantasy world of polluted water and monstrous creatures that slithered out of some noxious netherworld. But they weren't just the fantastical dreams of a young mind.

They were premonitions.

Silver had spent his youth and his teenage years honing his skills of manipulation. Through sheer will and intensified fellness, he took down anyone who was in his way. Providence was always on his side.

By adulthood he'd amassed a great fortune not only in monetary terms but in pure, tenebrous knowledge. Thousands of ancient texts, clay tablets, animal skins, human flesh tomes: all of it collected and studied by Silver until he knew everything he needed to know.

So now he stood on the stage, looking out onto the Atlantic Ocean where the city of R'lyeh had risen like a jade erection preparing to fuck the world into oblivion.

Silver snickered again.

He grabbed the pages of the *Abrund Abschaum* he had torn from Paulo's body and started to read them into the microphone. He knew the text would come to him somehow. He had always known it would come. The audience sat enraptured, their brains and bodies buzzing in a meditative haze. They would soon realize that they had had the same dreams as he, except that in theirs they were simply pawns of the new world, fodder for an ancient machinery that had finally come back to life.

Silver looked at Enzo who was sobbing into his hands. No doubt his brain was spinning with insanity. He was weak and unprepared to understand pure unadulterated knowledge.

Silver read all fifty-two pages of the text. He watched the audience stand up from their seats and slowly walk down to the beach. Oh, how happy he was to see them wading in the water, waiting for his instructions.

"You simple-minded servitors. Now you walk," he said, dropping the microphone in order to bask in this final glory.

Behind him, Enzo fell to the ground, his bones having turned to jelly. In front of him both Cop and Slave were having violent seizures that ended suddenly as their milky eyes popped out of their skulls and their ribs broke from their chests.

At that moment, Silver knew something had gone wrong.

His mouth, which had once snickered with anticipation, was now frowning with horror. He could feel it around him, vibrating through multiple dimensions. But this wasn't supposed to happen. This wasn't like his dreams.

Was there a part of the dream from his childhood that he had forgotten?

It didn't matter. Silver stood there on the stage, watching the stupefied audience, those passive spectators as they walked through the water towards R'lyeh. And if they had turned back to see their once revered entertainer, they would have seen him express a silent scream of agony as he was devoured by an invisible abomination.

Within seconds, there was nothing left.

Nothing at all.

ABOUT THE AUTHOR

Jordan Krall writes bizarro, horror, crime fiction, and apocalyptic literature. His books include *Fistful of Feet* and *Beyond the Valley of the Apocalypse Donkeys*. You may contact him at http://jordankrall.wordpress.com.

Bizarro books

CATALOG SPRING 2011

Bizarro Books publishes under the following imprints:

www.rawdogscreamingpress.com

www.eraserheadpress.com

www.afterbirthbooks.com

www.swallowdownpress.com

For all your Bizarro needs visit:

WWW.BIZARROCENTRAL.COM

Introduce yourselves to the bizarro fiction genre and all of its authors with the Bizarro Starter Kit series. Each volume features short novels and short stories by ten of the leading bizarro authors, designed to give you a perfect sampling of the genre for only $10.

BB-0X1
"The Bizarro Starter Kit" (Orange)

Featuring D. Harlan Wilson, Carlton Mellick III, Jeremy Robert Johnson, Kevin L Donihe, Gina Ranalli, Andre Duza, Vincent W. Sakowski, Steve Beard, John Edward Lawson, and Bruce Taylor. **236 pages $10**

BB-0X2
"The Bizarro Starter Kit" (Blue)

Featuring Ray Fracalossy, Jeremy C. Shipp, Jordan Krall, Mykle Hansen, Andersen Prunty, Eckhard Gerdes, Bradley Sands, Steve Aylett, Christian TeBordo, and Tony Rauch. **244 pages $10**

BB-0X2
"The Bizarro Starter Kit" (Purple)

Featuring Russell Edson, Athena Villaverde, David Agranoff, Matthew Revert, Andrew Goldfarb, Jeff Burk, Garrett Cook, Kris Saknussemm, Cody Goodfellow, and Cameron Pierce **264 pages $10**

BB-001"The Kafka Effekt" D. Harlan Wilson - A collection of forty-four irreal short stories loosely written in the vein of Franz Kafka, with more than a pinch of William S. Burroughs sprinkled on top. **211 pages $14**

BB-002 "Satan Burger" Carlton Mellick III - The cult novel that put Carlton Mellick III on the map ... Six punks get jobs at a fast food restaurant owned by the devil in a city violently overpopulated by surreal alien cultures. **236 pages $14**

BB-003 "Some Things Are Better Left Unplugged" Vincent Sakwoski - Join The Man and his Nemesis, the obese tabby, for a nightmare roller coaster ride into this postmodern fantasy. **152 pages $10**

BB-004 "Shall We Gather At the Garden?" Kevin L Donihe - Donihe's Debut novel. Midgets take over the world, The Church of Lionel Richie vs. The Church of the Byrds, plant porn and more! **244 pages $14**

BB-005 "Razor Wire Pubic Hair" Carlton Mellick III - A genderless humandildo is purchased by a razor dominatrix and brought into her nightmarish world of bizarre sex and mutilation. **176 pages $11**

BB-006 "Stranger on the Loose" D. Harlan Wilson - The fiction of Wilson's 2nd collection is planted in the soil of normalcy, but what grows out of that soil is a dark, witty, otherworldly jungle... **228 pages $14**

BB-007 "The Baby Jesus Butt Plug" Carlton Mellick III - Using clones of the Baby Jesus for anal sex will be the hip sex fetish of the future. **92 pages $10**

BB-008 "Fishyfleshed" Carlton Mellick III - The world of the past is an illogical flatland lacking in dimension and color, a sick-scape of crispy squid people wandering the desert for no apparent reason. **260 pages $14**

BB-009 **"Dead Bitch Army" Andre Duza** - Step into a world filled with racist teenagers, cannibals, 100 warped Uncle Sams, automobiles with razor-sharp teeth, living graffiti, and a pissed-off zombie bitch out for revenge. **344 pages $16**

BB-010 **"The Menstruating Mall" Carlton Mellick III** - "The Breakfast Club meets Chopping Mall as directed by David Lynch." - Brian Keene **212 pages $12**

BB-011 **"Angel Dust Apocalypse" Jeremy Robert Johnson** - Methheads, man-made monsters, and murderous Neo-Nazis. "Seriously amazing short stories..." - Chuck Palahniuk, author of Fight Club **184 pages $11**

BB-012 **"Ocean of Lard" Kevin L Donihe / Carlton Mellick III** - A parody of those old Choose Your Own Adventure kid's books about some very odd pirates sailing on a sea made of animal fat. **176 pages $12**

BB-015 **"Foop!" Chris Genoa** - Strange happenings are going on at Dactyl, Inc, the world's first and only time travel tourism company. "A surreal pie in the face!" - Christopher Moore **300 pages $14**

BB-020 **"Punk Land" Carlton Mellick III** - In the punk version of Heaven, the anarchist utopia is threatened by corporate fascism and only Goblin, Mortician's sperm, and a blue-mohawked female assassin named Shark Girl can stop them. **284 pages $15**

BB-021**"Pseudo-City" D. Harlan Wilson** - Pseudo-City exposes what waits in the bathroom stall, under the manhole cover and in the corporate boardroom, all in a way that can only be described as mind-bogglingly irreal. **220 pages $16**

BB-023 **"Sex and Death In Television Town" Carlton Mellick III** - In the old west, a gang of hermaphrodite gunslingers take refuge from a demon plague in Telos: a town where its citizens have televisions instead of heads. **184 pages $12**

BB-027 **"Siren Promised" Jeremy Robert Johnson & Alan M Clark**
- Nominated for the Bram Stoker Award. A potent mix of bad drugs, bad dreams, brutal bad guys, and surreal/incredible art by Alan M. Clark. **190 pages $13**

BB-030 **"Grape City" Kevin L. Donihe** - More Donihe-style comedic bizarro about a demon named Charles who is forced to work a minimum wage job on Earth after Hell goes out of business. **108 pages $10**

BB-031**"Sea of the Patchwork Cats" Carlton Mellick III** - A quiet dreamlike tale set in the ashes of the human race. For Mellick enthusiasts who also adore The Twilight Zone. **112 pages $10**

BB-032 **"Extinction Journals" Jeremy Robert Johnson** - An uncanny voyage across a newly nuclear America where one man must confront the problems associated with loneliness, insane dieties, radiation, love, and an ever-evolving cockroach suit with a mind of its own. **104 pages $10**

BB-034 **"The Greatest Fucking Moment in Sports" Kevin L. Donihe**
- In the tradition of the surreal anti-sitcom Get A Life comes a tale of triumph and agape love from the master of comedic bizarro. **108 pages $10**

BB-035 **"The Troublesome Amputee" John Edward Lawson** - Disturbing verse from a man who truly believes nothing is sacred and intends to prove it. **104 pages $9**

BB-037 **"The Haunted Vagina" Carlton Mellick III** - It's difficult to love a woman whose vagina is a gateway to the world of the dead. **132 pages $10**

BB-042 **"Teeth and Tongue Landscape" Carlton Mellick III** - On a planet made out of meat, a socially-obsessive monophobic man tries to find his place amongst the strange creatures and communities that he comes across. **110 pages $10**

BB-043 **"War Slut" Carlton Mellick III** - Part "1984," part "Waiting for Godot," and part action horror video game adaptation of John Carpenter's "The Thing." **116 pages $10**

BB-045 **"Dr. Identity" D. Harlan Wilson** - Follow the Dystopian Duo on a killing spree of epic proportions through the irreal postcapitalist city of Bliptown where time ticks sideways, artificial Bug-Eyed Monsters punish citizens for consumer-capitalist lethargy, and ultraviolence is as essential as a daily multivitamin. **208 pages $15**

BB-047 **"Sausagey Santa" Carlton Mellick III** - A bizarro Christmas tale featuring Santa as a piratey mutant with a body made of sausages. 124 pages $10

BB-048 **"Misadventures in a Thumbnail Universe" Vincent Sakowski** - Dive deep into the surreal and satirical realms of neo-classical Blender Fiction, filled with television shoes and flesh-filled skies. **120 pages $10**

BB-049 **"Vacation" Jeremy C. Shipp** - Blueblood Bernard Johnson leaved his boring life behind to go on The Vacation, a year-long corporate sponsored odyssey. But instead of seeing the world, Bernard is captured by terrorists, becomes a key figure in secret drug wars, and, worse, doesn't once miss his secure American Dream. **160 pages $14**

BB-053 **"Ballad of a Slow Poisoner" Andrew Goldfarb** Millford Mutterwurst sat down on a Tuesday to take his afternoon tea, and made the unpleasant discovery that his elbows were becoming flatter. **128 pages $10**

BB-055 **"Help! A Bear is Eating Me" Mykle Hansen** - The bizarro, heartwarming, magical tale of poor planning, hubris and severe blood loss...
150 pages $11

BB-056 **"Piecemeal June" Jordan Krall** - A man falls in love with a living sex doll, but with love comes danger when her creator comes after her with crab-squid assassins. **90 pages $9**

BB-058 **"The Overwhelming Urge" Andersen Prunty** - A collection of bizarro tales by Andersen Prunty. **150 pages** **$11**

BB-059 **"Adolf in Wonderland" Carlton Mellick III** - A dreamlike adventure that takes a young descendant of Adolf Hitler's design and sends him down the rabbit hole into a world of imperfection and disorder. **180 pages** **$11**

BB-061 **"Ultra Fuckers" Carlton Mellick III** - Absurdist suburban horror about a couple who enter an upper middle class gated community but can't find their way out. **108 pages $9**

BB-062 **"House of Houses" Kevin L. Donihe** - An odd man wants to marry his house. Unfortunately, all of the houses in the world collapse at the same time in the Great House Holocaust. Now he must travel to House Heaven to find his departed fiancee. **172 pages** **$11**

BB-064 **"Squid Pulp Blues" Jordan Krall** - In these three bizarro-noir novellas, the reader is thrown into a world of murderers, drugs made from squid parts, deformed gun-toting veterans, and a mischievous apocalyptic donkey. **204 pages $12**

BB-065 **"Jack and Mr. Grin" Andersen Prunty** - "When Mr. Grin calls you can hear a smile in his voice. Not a warm and friendly smile, but the kind that seizes your spine in fear. You don't need to pay your phone bill to hear it. That smile is in every line of Prunty's prose." - Tom Bradley. **208 pages $12**

BB-066 **"Cybernetrix" Carlton Mellick III** - What would you do if your normal everyday world was slowly mutating into the video game world from Tron? **212 pages** **$12**

BB-072 **"Zerostrata" Andersen Prunty** - Hansel Nothing lives in a tree house, suffers from memory loss, has a very eccentric family, and falls in love with a woman who runs naked through the woods every night. **144 pages $11**

BB-073 **"The Egg Man" Carlton Mellick III** - It is a world where humans reproduce like insects. Children are the property of corporations, and having an enormous ten-foot brain implanted into your skull is a grotesque sexual fetish. Mellick's industrial urban dystopia is one of his darkest and grittiest to date. **184 pages $11**

BB-074 **"Shark Hunting in Paradise Garden" Cameron Pierce** - A group of strange humanoid religious fanatics travel back in time to the Garden of Eden to discover it is infested with hundreds of giant flying man-eating sharks. **150 pages $10**

BB-075 **"Apeshit" Carlton Mellick III** - Friday the 13th meets Visitor Q. Six hipster teens go to a cabin in the woods inhabited by a deformed killer. An incredibly fucked-up parody of B-horror movies with a bizarro slant. **192 pages $12**

BB-076 **"Fuckers of Everything on the Crazy Shitting Planet of the Vomit At mosphere" Mykle Hansen** - Three bizarro satires. Monster Cocks, Journey to the Center of Agnes Cuddlebottom, and Crazy Shitting Planet. **228 pages $12**

BB-077 **"The Kissing Bug" Daniel Scott Buck** - In the tradition of Roald Dahl, Tim Burton, and Edward Gorey, comes this bizarro anti-war children's story about a bohemian conenose kissing bug who falls in love with a human woman. **116 pages $10**

BB-078 **"MachoPoni" Lotus Rose** - It's My Little Pony... *Bizarro* style! A long time ago Poniworld was split in two. On one side of the Jagged Line is the Pastel Kingdom, a magical land of music, parties, and positivity. On the other side of the Jagged Line is Dark Kingdom inhabited by an army of undead ponies. **148 pages $11**

BB-079 **"The Faggiest Vampire" Carlton Mellick III** - A Roald Dahl-esque children's story about two faggy vampires who partake in a mustache competition to find out which one is truly the faggiest. **104 pages $10**

BB-080 **"Sky Tongues" Gina Ranalli** - The autobiography of Sky Tongues, the biracial hermaphrodite actress with tongues for fingers. Follow her strange life story as she rises from freak to fame. **204 pages $12**

BB-081 "Washer Mouth" Kevin L. Donihe - A washing machine becomes human and pursues his dream of meeting his favorite soap opera star. **244 pages $11**

BB-082 "Shatnerquake" Jeff Burk - All of the characters ever played by William Shatner are suddenly sucked into our world. Their mission: hunt down and destroy the real William Shatner. **100 pages $10**

BB-083 "The Cannibals of Candyland" Carlton Mellick III - There exists a race of cannibals that are made of candy. They live in an underground world made out of candy. One man has dedicated his life to killing them all. **170 pages $11**

BB-084 "Slub Glub in the Weird World of the Weeping Willows" Andrew Goldfarb - The charming tale of a blue glob named Slub Glub who helps the weeping willows whose tears are flooding the earth. There are also hyenas, ghosts, and a voodoo priest **100 pages $10**

BB-085 "Super Fetus" Adam Pepper - Try to abort this fetus and he'll kick your ass! **104 pages $10**

BB-086 "Fistful of Feet" Jordan Krall - A bizarro tribute to spaghetti westerns, featuring Cthulhu-worshipping Indians, a woman with four feet, a crazed gunman who is obsessed with sucking on candy, Syphilis-ridden mutants, sexually transmitted tattoos, and a house devoted to the freakiest fetishes. **228 pages $12**

BB-087 "Ass Goblins of Auschwitz" Cameron Pierce - It's Monty Python meets Nazi exploitation in a surreal nightmare as can only be imagined by Bizarro author Cameron Pierce. **104 pages $10**

BB-088 "Silent Weapons for Quiet Wars" Cody Goodfellow - "This is high-end psychological surrealist horror meets bottom-feeding low-life crime in a techno-thrilling science fiction world full of Lovecraft and magic..." -John Skipp **212 pages $12**

BB-089 "Warrior Wolf Women of the Wasteland" Carlton Mellick III
Road Warrior Werewolves versus McDonaldland Mutants...post-apocalyptic fiction has never been quite like this. **316 pages $13**

BB-090 "Cursed" Jeremy C Shipp - The story of a group of characters who believe they are cursed and attempt to figure out who cursed them and why. A tale of stylish absurdism and suspenseful horror. **218 pages $15**

BB-091 "Super Giant Monster Time" Jeff Burk - A tribute to choose your own adventures and Godzilla movies. Will you escape the giant monsters that are rampaging the fuck out of your city and shit? Or will you join the mob of alien-controlled punk rockers causing chaos in the streets? What happens next depends on you. **188 pages $12**

BB-092 "Perfect Union" Cody Goodfellow - "Cronenberg's THE FLY on a grand scale: human/insect gene-spliced body horror, where the human hive politics are as shocking as the gore." -John Skipp. **272 pages $13**

BB-093 "Sunset with a Beard" Carlton Mellick III - 14 stories of surreal science fiction. **200 pages $12**

BB-094 "My Fake War" Andersen Prunty - The absurd tale of an unlikely soldier forced to fight a war that, quite possibly, does not exist. It's Rambo meets Waiting for Godot in this subversive satire of American values and the scope of the human imagination. **128 pages $11**

BB-095 "Lost in Cat Brain Land" Cameron Pierce - Sad stories from a surreal world. A fascist mustache, the ghost of Franz Kafka, a desert inside a dead cat. Primordial entities mourn the death of their child. The desperate serve tea to mysterious creatures. A hopeless romantic falls in love with a pterodactyl. And much more. **152 pages $11**

BB-096 "The Kobold Wizard's Dildo of Enlightenment +2" Carlton Mellick III - A Dungeons and Dragons parody about a group of people who learn they are only made up characters in an AD&D campaign and must find a way to resist their nerdy teenaged players and retarded dungeon master in order to survive. 232 **pages $12**

BB-097 **"My Heart Said No, but the Camera Crew Said Yes!" Bradley Sands -** A collection of short stories that are crammed with the delightfully odd and the scurrilously silly. **140 pages $13**

BB-098 **"A Hundred Horrible Sorrows of Ogner Stump" Andrew Goldfarb -** Goldfarb's acclaimed comic series. A magical and weird journey into the horrors of everyday life. **164 pages $11**

BB-099 **"Pickled Apocalypse of Pancake Island" Cameron Pierce** A demented fairy tale about a pickle, a pancake, and the apocalypse. **102 pages $8**

BB-100 **"Slag Attack" Andersen Prunty -** Slag Attack features four visceral, noir stories about the living, crawling apocalypse. A slag is what survivors are calling the slug-like maggots raining from the sky, burrowing inside people, and hollowing out their flesh and their sanity. **148 pages $11**

BB-101 **"Slaughterhouse High" Robert Devereaux -** A place where schools are built with secret passageways, rebellious teens get zippers installed in their mouths and genitals, and once a year, on that special night, one couple is slaughtered and the bits of their bodies are kept as souvenirs. **304 pages $13**

BB-102 **"The Emerald Burrito of Oz" John Skipp & Marc Levinthal** OZ IS REAL! Magic is real! The gate is really in Kansas! And America is finally allowing Earth tourists to visit this weird-ass, mysterious land. But when Gene of Los Angeles heads off for summer vacation in the Emerald City, little does he know that a war is brewing...a war that could destroy both worlds. **280 pages $13**

BB-103 **"The Vegan Revolution... with Zombies" David Agranoff** When there's no more meat in hell, the vegans will walk the earth. **160 pages $11**

BB-104 **"The Flappy Parts" Kevin L Donihe -** Poems about bunnies, LSD, and police abuse. You know, things that matter. **132 pages $11**

BB-105 "Sorry I Ruined Your Orgy" Bradley Sands - Bizarro humorist Bradley Sands returns with one of the strangest, most hilarious collections of the year. 130 pages $11

BB-106 "Mr. Magic Realism" Bruce Taylor - Like Golden Age science fiction comics written by Freud, *Mr. Magic Realism* is a strange, insightful adventure that spans the furthest reaches of the galaxy, exploring the hidden caverns in the hearts and minds of men, women, aliens, and biomechanical cats. **152 pages $11**

BB-107 "Zombies and Shit" Carlton Mellick III - "Battle Royale" meets "Return of the Living Dead." Mellick's bizarro tribute to the zombie genre. **308 pages $13**

BB-108 "The Cannibal's Guide to Ethical Living" Mykle Hansen - Over a five star French meal of fine wine, organic vegetables and human flesh, a lunatic delivers a witty, chilling, disturbingly sane argument in favor of eating the rich.. **184 pages $11**

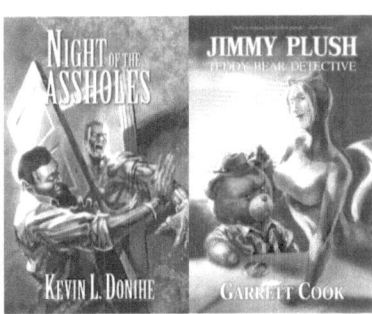

BB-109 "Starfish Girl" Athena Villaverde - In a post-apocalyptic underwater dome society, a girl with a starfish growing from her head and an assassin with sea anenome hair are on the run from a gang of mutant fish men. **160 pages $11**

BB-110 "Lick Your Neighbor" Chris Genoa - Mutant ninjas, a talking whale, kung fu masters, maniacal pilgrims, and an alcoholic clown populate Chris Genoa's surreal, darkly comical and unnerving reimagining of the first Thanksgiving. **303 pages $13**

BB-111 "Night of the Assholes" Kevin L. Donihe - A plague of assholes is infecting the countryside. Normal everyday people are transforming into jerks, snobs, dicks, and douchebags. And they all have only one purpose: to make your life a living hell.. **192 pages $11**

BB-112 "Jimmy Plush, Teddy Bear Detective" Garrett Cook - Hard-boiled cases of a private detective trapped within a teddy bear body. **180 pages $11**

COMING SOON

Tumor Fruit by Carlton Mellick III

Space Walrus by Kevin L. Donihe

Walrus Tales edited by Kevin L. Donihe

Porn Land by Kevin Shamel

Unicorn Battle Squad by Kirsten Alene

Dodgeball High by Bradley Sands

www.ingramcontent.com/pod-product-compliance
Lightning Source LLC
Chambersburg PA
CBHW020837260626
47169CB00003B/1036